CIRCUIT

CIRCUIT

a novella

James Berry

*For Imre
and Mrs. Truswell*

I died looking for big dick. Huge cock. Thick length. Girth. Everyone who's anyone in London these days, those who knew me, they knew that I was after hung guys. I was a "delight to have in class" who, two decades later, fell into the canyon between doormat and great friend. Hard corners like Ikea furniture carpeted over with modest stubble, eyes like black-ringed opals dropped from high into milk. Five ten. All this, indisputable, if you asked around. And with that, had you dropped your head between lumberjack shoulders in the Brewers on a Saturday night and asked, had you wandered into the 7.15AM HIIT class in Vauxhall on Thursday mornings and shouted over the trainer pacing between benches, had you gone to Dean Street Townhouse, into the nook at the back, on a Sunday afternoon and enquired above the hodgepodge of roasts and eggs, had you asked about me, the gospel would preach: size queen.

Predictable, then. No, not a great asset or quality in a person, but not the worst thing to be either. Like being vegan or calling oneself *sapiosexual*. And it hadn't ever hindered me, in the long run. I was never cruel about it; if I found myself in a situation where we both dropped trou', I would never have been mean or judgemental. I would do the noble thing: I would top. I can top in an emergency, a fifteen minute gym shower affair when the protein shake kicks in too early, or in the bathroom of a cocktail bar when I'm idling alone in the hour it takes for the grime and tedium of work to slough off of my skin and I am gearing myself up for a night sweating in the dirty mist and neon of Soho. Or in cases when I'm confronted with a man, a perfectly perfunctory partner, with all the bells and whistles but whose whistles seems to be, for me, decidedly lacking. So I can top.

Exhibit number one: the blissed-out mewling of the man whose hole I've taken care of in the apartment somewhere between the Thames and Camberwell. Just one trainer left to put on, already clad in my jacket again, he rolls on his peach bedsheets, writhing dramatically in the post-coital glow. He's naked still, and I can see a patch on the bed halfway down that tells me I'm still leaking out of him. I grin a self-satisfied knot as I lean over to spank his ass. Tell him thanks as he paws at me for one more round. I consult my watch and see I've got fifteen minutes until fashionably late becomes plain rude, before people start missing me. "Fifteen you can fuck me in again, you mean." A kiss, a tug, and I flee.

I beat across Black Prince Road, making my way through bruisey darkness, across residential streets filled with families winding down for the night and young revellers getting ready to begin. Rainbow flags fly from every building here, more so than usual, a plethora of them, a myriad, as Pride approaches tomorrow and the festivities begin. Not an hour has passed all day without a text message or DM from some head-nod acquaintance from Clapham or chemistry-riddled session drenched by steam and sweat:

> *What you up to for Pride?*
> *What's the motive?*
> *What you saying, handsome?*

I'm drowning in eggplants and devils.

"Fuck!" I collide with a body, shoulder to shoulder, and swing around with juvenile instinct. I'm face to face with six feet two of runway model mixed with a little bit of homeless chic. Looking like a billboard for every fashion brand out there, he sports a tattoo of a wolf's head on his tanned neck. He looks at me with irritation and disdain before readjusting his wireless earphones and ploughing on. I stand like a lemon for a beat longer. I roll my eyes, shrug my jacket back into proper position on my shoulders.

I pass a coffee shop near Little Portugal, its terrace populated with the older glitterati types, sun-wrinkled in cargo shorts and polo shirts, sipping the dregs of lattes purchased hours prior whilst waxing and lamenting between one another. I'm making good time as I walk a half-beat faster than the average hetero, and in this distance, like a syringe stabbed into the pavement,

I see Jared's building piercing the skyline before me: the Needle.

A few hours earlier, my vantage has me on the stationary bike on the mezzanine. In sweatpants and a hoody, baseball cap and Vans, I see the scene play out on the gym floor before. I play guardian angel from my perch, only half-listening to the Gen Y nostalgia soundtrack invading my ears. I nod to the odd guy who makes eye contact as I pump and cycle, men I know from either the steam room or spin class.

I plough on. I consult my watch. I've been cycling for twenty minutes, and still another forty to go if I want to keep the self-hatred in deficit. I smell, I know I do. I read somewhere that if you can smell yourself a little, other people can smell you a lot. I say a brief mantra that my scent is being cushioned by the hoody. A mantra, because I gave up the Church, capital C, and with it, prayer, after I left Lancashire a decade ago before moving here. So now I have mantras. Meditations for the day that sometimes are churned out with a buzz at 6.30 AM routinely, flashing up on my home screen as I awaken to scheduled wind chimes and the morning news purring from the little speaker that rests by my desk. *Today's theme is: water off a duck's back.* Minutes later when I'm needling the pre-Me, the just-awakened Bear, trying to do damage control on the meagre sleep and the gin and Café Patrón I can smell on my fingertips, in my stubble, on my tongue from the night before, I parrot back these words, these daily mottos, at my rough, unprepared face in hopes that they will marry the serums and moisturisers and BB cream.

6PM arrives and I find myself baking in the dim sauna, my towel rolled up just an inch more than standard, as the changing room begins to swell with people who weren't able to duck out early enough from work. I know the gym floor will thicken with bodies now, every machine taken over, queues for the Smiths and squat rack. I relax further, sink into the cedar wood, as I feel salty beads plop off my nose like full stops. I try to roll the knots out of my back, the angel wings tattoo there undulating with the movements of my scapula. My legs still wobble slightly as the exhaustion from the cardio threatens to catch up.

Enter Claudio. Freelancer Claudio, using that word liberally and generously, getting the full elastic stretch out of it given the many hats he wears. Sweat-drenched and slick post-bootcamp, a slight variation on the cookie-cutter cornfed US immigrant I see on social media. He looks like he would be in a comic film parody, one of those B-movies that come to supermarkets in DVD before the blockbuster. Skin-fade with a crown of blond thorns, he blue-steels his way in, delts first as he sashays. His towel would not have passed the fingertips test back at St. Seb's. He catches my eye, nods a little, sits on the row across from me. Rolls his neck, leans his head back with a small thud against the wood. Spreads.

"Hey man." He speaks like he's been screaming all day, sounds like old Hollywood, golden Westerns pushed through slightly Botoxed lips. I can't draw my eyes from his chest, the peach gloss of his skin. His mouth is parted, his breathing deep.

"Hey Claudio," I say, trying to affect some nonchalance. Claudio is a different kind of cool down fun, if I can get it. "Good sesh?"

"You know what it's like." Another neck roll. Adjusts himself under the towel. He parts his eyes slightly, squints, looks baked. "I had Amir. He's a bastard when he leads the class." The patter continues back and forth for a minute and change. Then: an eyebrow quirk. "So what's the plan for the weekend?"

I smile. "Hedonism. Just want to get drunk and messy and be naughty." Hands on my thighs, my knee twitching once. I scootch around a little, so Claudio and I are on a right angle. He quirks open an eye, follows me. Smirks. "What about you?"

"Busy time for me." Obviously, he only asked because he wanted to talk. Like all gays, like myself. "Few clients, I'm dancing tonight at Glitch." Can't help but wonder how much heavy lifting the word *dancing* is doing there. "Saturday, we're all heading east for brunch." A feline stretch as his napkin of a towel moves perilously. "I always overbook myself during Pride."

"I know what you mean. I've got a few mates coming in from Manchester, Leeds, Bristol." I don't; all my friends live in the same three-mile radius. "Don't know how I'm gonna get around to see them all, 'cause they're all planning on ending up different parties."

"Just make sure you end up at Glitch." I follow a bead of sweat, pearlescent with salt and grime from skin exposed to the city, meander down Claudio's front. I witness it in HD, ten eighty. It leaves a snail's trail which catches the light shining in from the changing room, disappears into the fibres of cloth resting on his hips. "I'll put you on the guest list if you want."

I swallow. "Yeah, I was planning on Glitch anyway. Got VIP tickets." I catch his glance again, hooded lids. He closes his eyes once more, wriggles a little in place. I can see his arousal plastered between his towel and his thigh. See one corner of this mouth quirk as he feigns an itch between his legs. I'm getting hard too, could swear I can feel blood descending from my ears, beelining to my crotch. My legs still pulse with my workout catching up with me, but my libido is winning out. I adjust myself over my towel, scratch the side of my nose. I can almost see myself third person, on high, like some judgemental ancestor.

Is that … is that an attempt at nonchalance?

My arms on the back of the bench. My eyes flit between the clear door, condensation dappling the glass, and Claudio, unmoving Claudio, save the slight tremor in one knee.

I move a moment closer. Drop my tone and register. "So—"

"Fuck, it's too hot in here." He gathers his towel around him - I think I see a flash of meat - and he pushes the door open. "See you at Glitch, handsome." A chill sweeps into the steam room, smothering all the heat. Goosebumps. Nipples harden.

"So, he just put on a show and then fucked off?"

Good old reliable Axel. Stalwart pillar into which I can bitch and moan and lament and vent. Sponge for all problems. He moved here more or less the same time as me, only whereas I travelled a couple hundred miles south, he traversed to London from Berlin. One foot rests on the coffee table before us, knee cocked out at an angle, he sits slovenly but like he's posing for a modelling gig in his head. Gin and tonic in one hand, the backs of his knuckles are slick with thawed ice.

He was two drinks in when I texted him to come down and get me, on number three as soon as we strode through the doors of Jared's apartment, so naturally, I threw back two shots that I saw on the open kitchen counter, one pastel and one neon, and ordered a double from some tanned twink I recognise from socials, Fabio or Andrea or something, who has situated himself behind the island. Drained it. It's Pride, fuck it. "I've booked Monday off," I say to Axel, winking to the Sardinian with a look in his eyes like sparked flint or fractured opals. He bites his bottom lip and begins to smirk. It's nice to get some recognition from us, the big boys.

Axel dragged me over to a corner, the last apparent empty seats in the lounge, his belonging splashed all over the corner, and immediately needled me for my weekend plans. A few seconds into my spiel, barely a toe over the starting line, you couldn't have even clocked it, I mentioned Claudio and his blue-balls antics. His cock-teasing. And thus, the outburst from Axel.

He continues, "I mean, that is just homophobic," And I slosh my highball around my wrist and my shoulder drops and the camp gets knocked up a notch. You're never as butch as when you're trying to get laid, they say, but I wasn't looking for a fuck right then. We get splashed with neon lights and the screech of pop princesses as the room begins to fill with a pick and mix of men that I vaguely know, or know carnally, or saw through filters and hashtags. I can smell the beginning of out-of-towners bleeding into the mix; can see the men and boys from Dubai, Barca, Mykonos, those who dropped their luggage off at the apart-hotel before beelining to wherever their phones deigned to be party central. And Jared threw a hell of a party.

The Needle lent itself to them. Fairly new, Scandi designed, filled with twenty-something City wankers to fifty-something TV moguls nearer the top. Jared hovered around the middle, figuratively, with a job as a lead producer on daytime TV, which afforded him some cachet amongst the young actors and the crowds of men all gunning for a chance to plug their business.

I knock back another swig of my drink, eyeing the crowd. South west corner of the room, the view is mighty perfect. I managed to dredge my gaze from the vista of the city and fix Axel back with a pleadingly naked stare. "Right?"

"I mean, if you're telling the whole truth? You didn't go into a cubicle with him?"

I recoil a little, not too much. "No!"

Andrew should be here, but I can't see him for the throngs, and Jared keeps flitting in my peripheral like a glitchy television. There are texts in my inbox stamped a few minutes ago from various people telling me they are on their way, which naturally means they won't have even left their flats yet. My phone is tentatively in my grasp, I'm toying with it on the periphery of the table. Axel isn't look at me, is staring over my shoulder at some fey-looking boy with mascara on and a confection of platinum hair. I've lost him, I can tell, momentarily, and so I drag my phone back into my view and check my texts, home screen blank. First time in hours. I close my eyes for a brief moment, sink into the cheap cushion, the pleather, the Chart Top 40s pop music.

"Bear!"

Axel looks exasperated. I shift a little, my drink spilling on my shirt accusatorially. "No, I fucking didn't go into the shower with him." I drain the rest of my gin and tonic, slam the glass on the marble tabletop. I move from mellow to defensive with a tensing of my shoulders and a firmness in my posture. Axel shuffles up to proper position, puts down his drink, wipes his hand on his jeans. "Fuck, I'm wound up."

"You messaged earlier saying you got some D during your lunch break?"

"Yeah? And I'm still wound up." I pick up my phone again, pointedly not mentioning the hook up I ducked into on the way here.

"Well, some of us don't have the luxury of getting dick on tap like you."

"Hardly on tap, Axel."

"Some of us are lucky to get laid once a week, and that's even with the apps."

"Don't be all feeling sorry for yourself, you've got cheekbones like glass and you dress better than any gay for a five-mile radius."

He pauses, folds into himself a little with an impish grin, like he sucked a lemon a little bit, like he's remembered an amusing joke from a few days ago. "Thank you, Bear. Quite possibly the nicest thing you've said to me."

"I *am* a nice guy."

"Are you though?"

We cackle, guttural; a shared cackle that undulates over the baseline and turns a couple of heads. I enjoy the idea of what they see, of the image I have of in my head, of the image of us in the head, and the narrative they must be fabricating, of martinis and Ubers and designer sample sales and coke-fuelled nights winding up in some penthouse overlooking the Thames every night.

Andrew floats over finally, bringing a couple of friends in tow. One is the fey twink at which Axel was making goo-goo eyes. Something like Brad but whose name is constantly being swallowed by the fabrics and the crush of bodies as the apartment begins to swell and the noise ricochets off of every surface around us. The other, Robbie, I know from head nods and Insta likes and cameo appearances in the backgrounds of mutual's photos. We like Robbie, who works in theatre and lives in West London, Acton or Ealing somewhere, and isn't super 'roided up, with bobbly skin like plucked chicken flesh, small red sores worn like badges of pride. Isn't vasc as fuck. Doesn't seem to care that his hairline is ebbing back like low tide. We like Robbie.

Another round of highballs fills the table, save a flute of champagne. "I only drink champagne," Thad says, sipping the glass in a fashion I'm certain he thinks is demure, thinks it paints him like Rita Hayworth or Veronica Lake. He's wearing lip gloss and he's had fillers, which, we don't judge, but I imagine he was in nursery during 9/11, so it makes me quirk my head, tilt and gaze as he speaks. I see Axel is living, his eyes glistening with mal intent, he's almost frothing at the possibility of fucking with Chad. I zone out within a few seconds of the beginning of his chatter, pivot to Andrew and Robbie.

"So what's the goss?"

Andrew turns to me. "Plan is not to get too messy."

"We *all* want to get messy, Drew." This from Jared, master at spinning many plates. He saunters over from a gaggle. Six foot tangerine with blue-white teeth, he embraces me in a one-armed hug, a drink in his other hand. He has sticky palms which hold onto gossip and facts like flypaper. He isn't exactly an alpha, but he does manage to keep everyone in his grasp like a ringmaster.

"Actually, some of us weren't lucky enough to get tomorrow off." Andrew takes a big gulp, suggestive ministrations of his Adam's apple on display in his shirt with too many buttons undone, his Mykonos tan a bright terracotta.

My brow furrows, my whole face laments. "Oh no, babe, no?"

"What do you *do*?" BradThad enquires with a note of disgust in his tone, a soupçon of pity. Andrew is a decade older and about thirty kilos heavier, in a good way, and knowledge of these two things make me want to throw my drink on this twink, who sits with crossed legs and a pinched face. Who the fuck invited him? Andrew isn't much of a glutton for punishment, despite what I know to be his domination kink. I stare wide-eyed at Jared, who runs a hand through his bleached hair, combs it behind his right ear. Fixes me with a similar stare, a raised eyebrow. *Who invited this dickhead?*

Andrew, ever the diplomat. "I work in events." He could have added *little one*, did when we first met, I'm

13

sure. "I'm lead on a big project over Pride weekend, so no fun for me until Sunday evening."

"*Fun*, eh?" From Robbie.

"I thought you got it off?" I ask.

"Our brave solider," Axel chimes, "Missing out on all the debauchery."

His lips form an em dash. "Mischa bailed." Eye roll. "Apparently, going into labour takes priority." A small smile and chuckle to himself, mirrored by us all.

From someone: "Bad luck."

"Well, you've done one Pride, you've done them all." This elicits knowing nods from us elders, memories from summer debuts spent at parties or in dark rooms. Rubbing aloe into our sunburnt lobster skins after stretches on the heath or by the lidos. From the youth – the twink with the slug lips, Jared who isn't too young but is still a half-decade our junior, from the couple of kids on the periphery who know one of us to through Facebook or Twitter and have half-slinked into the conversation with a *Heeeeeeey* – they look as though Andrew has blasphemed.

"Ain't that the truth." And I swig my second highball with gusto. The glass lands back on the table and clinks perilously with someone's champagne flute. I see Robbie leaning into the ear of one of the younger chaps, and the younger chap doing the same to him, and the youth gets up and heads to the kitchen.

I can feel the momentum of the gin kicking in. I missed dinner, or rather I chose not to eat in favour of feeding a more carnal urge, and between leaving my Berwick Street office and finishing my workout, all my stomach lining saw were a few breath mints and a protein bar. I'm not going to be the guy who suggests food before the club, but my fingers begin the journey across my phone screen to one of the takeaway apps with hazy desire and healthy apprehension. My empty hand finds its way to resting on my stomach, over my plain white shirt, a Dries, and pressing into my abs, as if reminding me, warning me, and I feel a wave of sadness, renewed hunger, loss, roil in my belly. I turn more towards to the table, to the group, to see if maybe there's another round being placed down. I see Jared, see him fixing me with a stare that tells me he's been talking a fair few seconds.

"What?" Immediately on the defensive.

"I was saying," a finger on the hand holding his drinking pointing square at me, "that we could do with a little shopping for tonight." A pause, a shrug. "A little motive."

Axel barks a laugh. "'*Motive*'? Who does she think she is?"

"Someone that actually lives in South London." Jared tilts his head at him. "Who are you?"

"Someone who doesn't pretentiously take on other dialects and then use words wrongly."

Police siren calls pass through the lips of a few of us around the table.

"Says the boy who sounds more like he's from Essex than Berlin."

15

"It's called Brexit, darling. Some of us have to assimilate for survival. I'm wounded that you voted Leave though." And as he leans over with puckered lips, baiting Jared with kissy noises, before Jared can spit out some comeback:

"Shots!" The kid whose ear had been in Robbie's mouth returns with a tray of shot glasses. The liquor within glows neon green, comic book toxic. Cheers from most as the sparring between Axel and Jared ceases for a beat. I find myself lamenting audibly in chorus with Andrew and Axel. Robbie plays hostess and begins passing around the drinks. I think of my empty stomach and feel a touch bilious as I take the glass and place it immediately on the table. I see Andrew has done the same, whilst Axel holds it aloft with reticence.

"Why do you have that in the flat?" Axel says churlishly to Jared, who doesn't take the bait.

"I'm not drinking that." Andrew says, and I back him up with a "Ditto." And yet, through raucous jeering and cries of protest against our protest, the countdown begins as each person present picks up their lime crime confection and, three two one, we all neck the battery acid. It tastes like a convulsion. Like someone in scrubs should have cried "Clear!" before I imbibed.

Face like he's chewing tin foil, Robbie places a slick glass back on the tray, turns to the guy who brought them over. "Thanks, Jase." A couple more coughed out splutters of thanks in his direction from Gen Z. Of course he's called Jason. I bet the other one who was idling by the table is called something like Chris or Craig or Shane.

"That was fucking gross." BradThadChad's voice is like fingernails now.

"Who's still buying bottles of sours in the year twenty-twenty?" This from Axel.

I turn to see Andrew pleasantly sipping his drink again, empty shot glass before him. My eyes are wide and he matches mine with fluttering eyelashes, innocence incarnate. I look between him and the shot. "What? Tastes like squash." Aussie lilt to his voice coming out bemused and coy.

I cry to the group, "So who's gonna get us some gear?"

Eyes fall on the extra, the day player. In his most diminutive voice: "I know a guy."

Someone says, "There's a good lad, Matty." And I grin to myself at my wrong assumption.

Our tongues are green and someone's bumped the music up another notch. The air is thickening steadily with cigarette smoke drifting in from the balcony overlooking Camberwell, with the cloying mottling of sweat and body heat. We're only a few doors down from the tube station, barely a minute's walk, although it can take five some nights from experience when you've got blood in your alcohol stream and no work the next day and you've been rejected by the few lads who you've tried it on with, the last of whom is only rejecting you because he's seen you throwing yourself with incrementally more vigour at men throughout the evening.

Hypothetically. Anecdotally, I hear

Face warm, neon dapples my vision. My wrist says 10PM. I am splayed against Axel, back to back. He chats with Matty and Jason, and I hear snatches of their conversation like passing cars over the music and white noise around us. I face Jared and Robbie, who are both talking about a new show opening on Shaftesbury in a few weeks. I'm barely following the conversation but enjoying the thrum of the evening as it pulls a wire through my body and tugs every now and again. I reach for my drink and find I don't have one, it's been cleared. I stand and wobble slightly.

"Alright, Bear?" Jared and Robbie have paused mid-conversation to look up at me. I see Andrew disappearing out the front door for a moment. ChadBradThad is nowhere I can see, and my smile creases the corners of my eyes.

My stomach cramps a little. I need to eat something soon. "I'm just gonna go get some cigs." I don't smoke unless I'm, as my mother would say, drunk as a skunk. I mainly use them as another weapon in my arsenal when I'm after a fuck. But I probably won't end up even buying any tonight. I just need to get some air and try and sober up a little bit. This weekend is poised to be a marathon, heavy, with blurred edges and hard bodies, but I'm not going to get through it if I don't pace myself.

Downstairs, on the street, I'm shocked a little by the drop from baking heat to the chill of British night time, and I flash back to the top deck of the number eighty-eight this time last year. Saturday afternoon, sun still decently poised, and I was so trashed I took myself home. Shirtless, a redness already beginning to spread across my shoulders and back like spilled Chianti. I developed a harness tan the next morning, having slept through the *Stallion* afterparty in Brixton until eleven AM.

Thirty pounds wasted.

Eighteen missed calls.

Double digit DMs.

Facepalm for days.

No photo evidence, thankfully. We have a rule that selfies have to be group-approved, so no embarrassment except for the second-hand tales I had recounted to me for days after. Axel telling me how I threw up on Soho Square, Andrew enjoying reminding me that, when he asked which gin I wanted, I said "Bacon and egg."

Not my finest.

I cringe as the 2PM feeling I felt last summer begins to announce itself again, as it had a year ago. I cross the road, dodging a black cab and a Routemaster, and huddle my coat closed a little more. I take out my phone and open up *Rendezdude*. The grid fills with stern faces, black profiles, ripped torsos, the odd landscape. I know most of them, as they populate the building behind me, I've been drinking with some of them for the past couple of hours. I see Axel's hard-planed face in a square next to my own, Robbie's wide smile outside some coffeeshop; I recognise Andrew's chest piece tattoo painted over his brioche bun pecs. Bottom middle row is occupied by Jared's lithe body, nautical stars mounted on both delts at the front. A couple of familiar faces in the mix too as I scroll but, from prior nights squandered in a booth at Glam Bar with my thumb working overkill, I can see the grid looks denser. Fresh meat in the mix. Pride has culled the country and brought all the acronyms to the capital, and all within a few streets of one another.

A hand falls on my shoulder, and I'm met with a broad smile of cemetery teeth, a meringue nest of dark curls, all attached to six feet of ex-boyfriend.

"Hello Bear," Nico pulls me in for a strong hug. A bear hug, if you will, which I willingly accept, the screen of my phone pressing in between my palm and his back. He's warm and comfy, like a soft fleece, and he smells like roses and pepper.

"Hey Nico," I pull back from the embrace like chewing gum leaving the pavement on the sole of a boot. He looks at me with glitter in his eyes, the disco lights of streetlamps across the road reflected in them. He looks between me and the Needle.

"Out here all alone?" The wind picks up around us and my shoulders bunch together, but Nico seems so chilled and calm as usual, in James Dean cosplay, white tee and black leather jacket. So solid, still, statuesque.

I am keenly aware of the descent of my eyelids but do nothing to open them wider. I slant a smile in his direction, teeth behind lips. "Just getting some of that fresh London air." I stop myself from fidgeting, resist the urge to seesaw between my feet. I look at the constellations of his face, think back to when we last spoke. It must've been a month ago at least, because I have no idea what he's up to this weekend. "I've peaked and I haven't eaten."

"You always forget to eat."

"Yes, *'forget.'*"

A raised eyebrow. "Please don't tell me you're on a diet."

"We don't all look like fashion models like you."

Deadpan. "You legitimately look like a fashion model."

"I'm five ten."

"Hardly a pocket gay. I'm not doing this."

We both let out gusts of amusement through toothy grins. His eyes scrunch a little, and I feel mine mirror.

"Who you with?" I ask, looking over his shoulder. Behind him, on the corner between this road and another, illuminated by the neon plastic of the corner shop, a couple of guys idle and look at our conversation. They look like Central St. Martin types, trench coats, bowl cuts, which pairs perfectly with Nico's bread and butter photography job.

He follows my sight line. "Just a couple of guys I've worked with. Thinking of hitting up Glitch later on but want to keep my stamina for the weekend." He looks between me and the bar. "What about you? You with Drew and Jare?"

"I have other friends, Nico."

"So Jared doesn't live in the Needle anymore and Andrew isn't in there, keeping your seat warm?"

A gust of wind punctuates the beat between us. I lick my lips.

Then, minutely: "Axel is there too."

Nico grins his harmonica smile, downcast eyes with origami folds at the corners. Another slap on my shoulder, the one furthest from him so I'm pulled again into his orbit, into his hug. Blink and you'll miss it, but it lasts long enough for me to feel the press of his St. Christopher against my cheek, for him to whisper into my temple, "You look good."

And then he's stepping away, walking backwards, eye contact locked in on me. There are a few people passing, the wind is performing a great monologue against the bricks and concrete around us, but he doesn't trip or err. "Have a good one, Bear!"

"You too, Nico," Swallowed by traffic, by tempest.

"I need to get *fucked*."

As soon as I'm back in Jared's apartment, I regroup the mafia and command someone make a firm plan. Within a minute or two of texts being sent out, we are all seated in the living space, phones in hand, coordinating with other tiers of friends who were far afield, streets away, in different bars, attempting to provide meat to the bones of our evening. We are waiting to hear back from one of Jared's current lays who is in a bar halfway en route to Rabbit Hole, a dive bar with a dark room at the back, when I notice my drink is empty.

To my left, Robbie heard me. "What you having?"

From someone: "Why don't we finish up here and head to Lucky's?"

"We need to get our asses to Glitch."

"We should hit up Nectar."

"We aren't going Glitch," from me.

Jared is barged out the way by two guys with backpacks: our dealer and his friend. They are making for the kitchen to lay out wares. "Excuse you." He consults his phone again. "Rodrigo says everyone is leaving the Hole and heading to a party out East."

"Effort."

"I'm not heading East."

"It doesn't feel like a Nectar night."

"I'm barred from Lucky's."

"So let's go Glitch."

Matty chimes, "There's a lot of people going to Valhalla."

A chorus of seethes, of low moans. Matty cringes.

From Jason, "What's wrong with Valhalla?"

"Our collective average age is about a decade too old to step foot in Valhalla."

"Nice pun."

Under his breath but loud enough for us all to hear, Jared says, "Speak for yourselves."

"What's wrong with Nectar?"

Andrew winces. "Nectar is a bit too … camp, don't you think?"

"Can *someone* make a decision? I'm sobering the fuck up." Axel's voice cuts through as he saunters off with a huff, glitter in his wake, cloud of Tom Ford in the space he vacated, to the kitchen. His wallet is coming out of his back pocket. At that moment, Robbie is back with drinks and a little baggie between his teeth. I take the glass from him on autopilot as we all watch the space left by Axel weaving through the crowd.

Finally, from Jared, "What's his damage?"

Robbie starts racking up a line on the coffee table before us with his bank card. It would be very performative from anybody else, but from Robbie, it's a little adorable, in all honesty. I drain clean half my highball and my phone vibrates. My heart swaps to spin cycle, rabbiting along as I check the screen for a notification from Nico. I turn slightly away from the group, who don't notice regardless, they're sucked in their own screens searching for the next move, Axel's minute tantrum forgotten. Except I glance a little, flutter my eyes northwards, see Robbie just being. No phone, no apparent motive, just leaning forward, inhaling like a hover, pinching his nose. People watching. I smile.

RendezDude alert. I collapse inwards a touch, bring the back of the hand holding my phone and press it for a beat between my eyes. Inhale. Feel my dick get hard as my heart goes soft. Press on the notification.

The message loads up from *HnHMikey*. I don't even bother to read, to look at the pictures. Tonight is not a high night for me, I don't want to blow my Pride load at the first hurdle. Another sip, more metaphors to mix.

I look at some of the older messages idling from the past couple of hours. The corner reads 10.48PM. I look over my shoulder at the guys, hear some generic sounds of a decision being made. I could duck out and find a warm body for thirty minutes or so, no one would miss me as we moved between venues. Options are thin on the ground if I don't want to wander too far a field; the grid isn't currently a plethora of talent, present company excluded, but my mind drifted southwards as soon as Nico clapped a warm hand on me. I've been thickening down there ever since.

Correspondence is brief with a guy with big traps, dark eyes, DSLs. Calls himself *ThiagoFun*, promises to be six feet three, has me doing math to figure out what twenty centimetres translates to.

I send Axel a brief note, *Gone hunting*, kiss emoji, peach emoji, water splash. "Right guys, so Glitch?" I've resigned myself as I move to get my coat from wherever I left it, lean over a couple who have now jumped in our graves to get them. Mumbled apologies. I look back at my friends, and the tagalongs, and feel the last drink settle warmly in my gut. Andrew eyes me funnily, he knows what's up, probably read over my shoulder a moment ago. A couple of looks from Robbie and Jared, just smiley, lemony acknowledgements of my presence.

I'm halfway down the road before my phone vibrates staccato.

Happy hunting, from Axel.

Don't waste the hole night, from Andrew. I smirk at his playfulness.

Cheers for bailing, face palm emoji. Jared can be a dick.

We don't even make it through his threshold. He buzzed me in, I walked up four flights of stairs, knocked on the door to his apart-hotel, and seconds later, my head is knocked upside the wall by the front door. His mouth is hot honey, his paws taking possession of every inch of my skin. He's all heat and sticky sweet candy, he tastes like the shots he's been doing. Tells me between foggy pants that he was at a bar, came home to shower, get ready for part two of his Friday night, has friends waiting for him in Soho somewhere, swallowed up by neon lights and vodka sodas. I mouth appropriate replies, grip his delts.

We are frantic, ravenous.

26

He's a unicorn, everything he promised to be and more. Pornstar body with a face like Italian films from the sixties, he speaks with Carnivale tones, with an accent conjuring tequila and sand, russet buildings and cartoon-blue beaches. He is naked, answered the door naked, with hooded dark eyes curtained behind unbridled curls the colour of treacle. My neck is wet with his tongue, and my jeans are still pooled around my ankles, his spit-slick fingers fishing in the back of my briefs. Our stubbles rub together Velcro-like, mine rough and London-weathered, his oil-soft. I shirk my shirt off, my jacket is already a puddle by the doorjamb, and I stomp out of my jeans.

He leads with fingers still inside me to the living space. The room is awash with electric blues and sharp pinks bleeding in from the windows. He only left on the track lighting underneath the cupboards by the kitchenette, most of the living room is a silhouette of itself. I moan against his mouth, waddling slightly as my briefs pause halfway down between my thighs. I rush to remove them, kick them into the middle of the room, but it's awkward going when there's a digit or two in your hole. It's erotic, but clumsy, but the kisses never stop, and my hands find his dick again, and it's thick and my fingers surround it, my smile growing wide as I continue meeting his lips with mine.

I clock the view immediately. We've barely batted five words between us but when I see the vista from the window, the orange juice strip of washi tape seven stories down from his building, the black cabs and buses all lined up leading down, past vape shops and corner shops and late night cafes, even Glitch down the road towards the roundabout, it pulls a comment out my throat before my mind has even completed it.

"Fuck me."

Agave voice seeps out like syrup. "I'm trying to,"

I say, "That view, though," and his fingers sluice out of me and his hand rests on my shoulder as he moves his mouth from the crook of my neck, turns to follow the path my eyes have taken. I glimpse his face, eyes glistening like marbled sorbet, whorls of tangerine and chocolate, but I'm drawn back to the road below, to the bustle of Vauxhall at night. I think I see a familiar head making his way towards the queue, flanked by two hipster mannequins, but I shake my head, scrunch my eyes up hard and look away. Admonish myself.

We stand, naked, dicks half-cocked, and I'm sobering up and missing my friends, but there's undiluted lust married to my blood at this moment and I'm thirsty for it, I'm hungry to be taken, to be used, to become the property of this man, Nico, no, Thiago, Thiago, if that's his real name, I'm not sure, we haven't swapped names yet. But I feel heady, woozy with arousal.

I turn back to him, begin kissing him again with more force. I fall through his lips sloppily. One of his hands is rough on the back of my head, the other palming my ass again, finding entrance. It's fast, it's frenetic, we move and act as though there's an imminent sex

28

recession, as if sex is water and we've been living in drought. I do not act as though I fucked only a few hours ago, and hours before that, and neither does he, and I'm certain he did because you don't look like that in London and not fuck on the regular.

And his dick tastes like poorly washed-off lube, I discover as I drop to my knees and take him in one go in my throat.

Blissful minutes pass, maybe even half an hour, elongated by his jackhammer thrusts into my skull. My jaw begins to ache, my knees needle the hardwood floor as we put on an unseen performance for the denizens beneath us. Night light carves his already chiselled body into moving sculpture. I look up through gags and grunts, my eyes foamy from choking, and take him all in, somehow growing even harder still, getting even more horny. He mewls ministrations, curses under his breath, indecipherable mutterings laced with alcohol and magic, his aggressive pounding ceaseless as he does. I'm euphoric, seeing glitter and lightning in my eyes as I slobber, and I do slobber, there's no lying about how enthusiastic I am. And I look up again, and Thiago looks down at me with pitchfork teeth and brown-fire eyes, looks at me like I'm a mess, and I drink it all in.

Cut to him lifting me from my position, hands under my armpits, now I'm standing, and he's turning me around and pressing me against the long tall window. Repositions me like a mannequin, kicks my ankle apart, bends me over double, does everything but ask me to

29

touch my toes without bending my knees. Plants a wet warm tongue between my cheeks and dark little artefacts blotch my vision. I feel myself shuddering and all hairs stand to attention. He chows down, runs a hand over my back from neck to tailbone, caresses my wings, the other hand milking me back to front. I'm going to draw blood; I'm kneading my lip raw with my teeth. I grunt out, "Stop teasing and fuck me." I'm going to explode any second.

I hear him stand. I don't turn around, don't want to break the spell of the twinkle of the grid below, London's patchwork, and the feel of him all over me, his scent on my mouth so strong I feel like there's a residue there, I feel claimed already, animalistic. He's in my nose, under my skin, and I need his shaft in me. I move my hand back behind me to try and guide it. He slaps it halfway past playfully. It goes straight to my dick.

"Now, now," he growls, and hefts me by my hips. I wiggle, I hope alluringly, but I know it's coming across desperate, but I can feel he needs to unload just as badly as I do. He doesn't even fetch any lube, I hear him spit, a wad of it, I swear I can hear it drip from his mouth, can picture it like a wet spider dropping into a cave from on high. He rubs some of it into my crack, and I clench and relax.

There it is, pressing into me from behind. And before me, in the distance, I see the crowd outside Glitch getting thicker, denser, even as I witness people going inside like a steady stream of lemmings. Fucking Pride tourists. Thunder cracks in my mind, something breaks within me. I'm being filled at one end and it's pushing out spit and nonsense at the other, babbling gibberish. Little packets of dynamite as he picks up pace, choo-choo-training my hole, the wet Mac and cheese slap of his thick quads against my cheeks. I feel the need to piss building in me, his hand around my dick jerking me closer to release. The slick of his sweat falling on my back from his curls. My hole tightens. My orgasm feels hot and dense and imminent.

My forehead keeps flopping against the window, a smudgy watermark from my own sweat spreading like a grease stain. Thiago is grunting, his throat is rollercoasting through peaks and valleys, and I can sense his orgasm is moments away. Mine is roiling behind my pubes, my bladder is screaming, all I can hear is the thudthudthud of my forehead and his raggedy breaths and the wet fish slap of our skin.

I see the flash before I hear the noise. The blue-black landscape that brings Gotham to mind is marred by a flash of an orange-white pulse in the centre of the roundabout at the bottom of the road below. A muffled gust and crackle and then a great big whoosh moving in tandem as a fireball the size of a lorry flies out the front of Glitch into the street, dredging with it the poor waiting denizens who seconds before were queueing for shots and mistakes. I see the behemoth explosion billow out, blowing back vehicles and cyclists, pedestrians and bouncers.

My body spikes with fear and ice and heat and piss and come and faces flood the every corner of my being, Axel's face, and Jared's, Robbie's bowling pin head and Andrew's lantern jaw and I can't cry because Thiago must have his eyes closed and his ears pinned shut because all I see is destruction raining from the nightclub at the end of the lane, thick clouds of misery avalanching misery into the street and he's fucking and fucking and fucking and then I feel myself coming and

I'm pumping a load into the hole, the now loose sphincter, of a man in an apartment behind Black Prince Road. I fall back slightly from the bed, from the nausea, a tumultuous wave of sickness and panic and I feel wrong, feel misplaced, like walking déja vu. My dick slips out of his hole, sliding free of warm tight muscle into the cooler air of the room, an air thick with sex and sweat, and I look down at his blissed-out body, the man from earlier tonight, last night, my mind can't process the dream I just lived, the evening I experienced. I can still feel a thickness in my own ass, my hole feels as though it is missing a phantom limb.

I fall back a little more, watch the last drains of my seed spill from the tip, and the man before me, posed doggy, falls like a dumped beanbag into the centre of his bed. His grey sheets are patchy with black smears, little globules of his own come haloing him like flecks of crime scene chalk. He rolls over, his chest hair matted and greasy with perspiration. His face is an ever-shifting mask of pleasure, and he finally locks eyes with me, through hooded lids, and pastes a smeary smile on the lower half of his face. Smug looking.

I can feel my own face frozen, a sheet of confusion, a crumpled piece of tan paper. I am on my haunches, then on my knees, and then twisting myself so I'm sitting off the bed. My egg white omelette and morning mass gainer threaten revolt as I descend from the high of my climax, and my vision stars to blur with vigour. And then I realise I'm beginning to weep, and I'm shaking, a tremor I can feel in my wrists and elbows. Barely, like I'm on a come down.

Blissed-out boy beside me rolls around a bit, ends up next to me, pawing at my arm. "That was fucking amazing." A small part of me that can't resist a joke or levity thinks *That's very generous of you* but I'd wager most of my brain functions are still set to red alert. Bred-bottom boy looks up at me and finally sees my face proper, matches my damp eyes to his dry ones, looks concerned. "You OK?"

I run the rough carpet of my forearm across my tears, shake my head. "I'm fine, always love to crymax." I fucking hate my automated wit sometimes. I scrunch my nose, actually slap my hands on my thighs like a tool, and get up, looking for my clothes. I don't look at the guy, can't, can feel him hovering on the edge of the bed, posed like Rose in *Titanic*. I beeline for my clothes, try to get out of my funk, this weird motion sickness I have roiling through my systems. I need to eat, settle my stomach, get somewhere. I'm meant to be somewhere. "What time is it?"

"Five minutes before you fuck me again," he replies, and after a few record-scratch moments flitter by, I'm up, shrugging off his beckoning fingertips and pulling up my jeans. My phone falls from my back pocket and I pick it up and consult the screen.

Friday, July 3rd. 20:48.

I should have been at Jared's at 8.30PM.

No, I was just there.

I press the back of my hand on the space between my eyes, scrunch them shut, and then reach for the rest of my clothes. I mumble apologies, mates are waiting, tell him the sex was good even though I can't remember anything except finishing inside him. I'm dressed in under a minute, lean over to give him a kiss on the forehead, and I'm out the door.

I beat down Black Prince Road, making my way through bruisey darkness, across residential streets filled with families winding down for the night and young revellers getting ready to begin. Rainbow flags fly from every building here, more so than usual, a plethora of –

"Fuck!" I collide with a body, shoulder to shoulder, and swing around with juvenile instinct. I'm face to face with six feet two of runway model mixed with a little bit of homeless chic. Looking like a billboard for every fashion brand out there, he sports a tattoo of a wolf's head on his tanned neck. He looks at me with irritation and disdain before readjusting his wireless earphones and ploughing on. I stand like a lemon for a beat longer, and the shakes begin anew. I vibrate and my stomach churns and I press my lips so hard I worry they'll spark like flint. I watch him walk away, the man from last night, my dream, my slip from reality into something so real I can still taste Thiago's musk and cologne.

I open my phone, load *RendezDude*. First row on the grid is home to the guy whose flat I've just vacated, and I go back into our DMs.

Did you give me chems?

I press send, staring at the little ticks. I worry my teeth will crack from the tension in my jaw. I watch him indirectly read the message, see ...*typing* pop up.

No? What the fuck?

I run a hand across my face, certain I'm drawing attention from those walking up and down the street, standing stock still and looking shell-shocked.

Must've been the other guy, I type out. Winky emoji and send.

A breath, a huff, and I head to the Needle.

Familiar faces dots the queue leading into Glitch. Hands are waved and heads are nodded as we pace a slow slog into the venue. *And this is for VIP ticket holders*, I think, doing brief, listless math about the on-the-door buyers, figure I'll run into one of them in a couple of hours at 2AM at the earliest. It's not too chilly, although chalk that up likely to the drinks nailed at Jared's and the can of G and T in my hand as we idle and shuffle closer to the door. I'm more relaxed now, the funk of my daydream sloughed off, and minutes later, we are scanning QR codes and dropping coats in the cloakroom. Being patted down my bouncers whose faces are familiar but whose names are a mystery.

"You feeling better now?" This from Andrew, who nudges my shoulder with his own as we beat down the corridor towards the club. "You seemed really low earlier."

"Yeah," I smile genuinely. "I just had a weird evening, was in a mood."

"You were *testy*. We thought you were on ket." Axel offers, breezing past us with Robbie in tow.

"Work?" Andrew asks.

"Work's great. Got a gig recording some new tracks for a radio drama. Solo."

"Impressive." He says, to my ego's satisfaction.

He takes my hand and we move, my eyes wandering like a magpie's. Axel and Robbie steaming ahead, carving a path through the thicket of bodies that stand between us and the main room. Jared is already inside. Axel is instantly accosted by two drag queens standing by one of the toilets, deep in conversation with flailing hands and hips on a metronome.

I take one last look back before we plunge into the room, falling victim to the remnant haze of a fog machine, to the sticky scent of cordials and cologne, of sweat and pleather, to the dominating thump of the party music. The tempo fills my body like bathwater and with every moment passing as we traverse the different levels, moving down further and further into the mosh pit of harnesses and narcotics, of muscle and vanity, the knots of worry that hours before had seemed so secure and tight and unshiftable are all but lost to the baseline.

Time must be partaking in the festivities tonight as it passes without comprehension or rhythm. I clock it as I blink and find myself at the bar with Andrew on my right and Robbie on my left and we throw back sambuca and chase it immediately with our drinks, and it feels like it's been a minute since we got into the venue but my shirt is off and so is Robbie's and good for him to have that kind of confidence. We move like eels through a swamp, hands resting like feathers on the lower backs of the men to signify we are trying to pass. Jared comes into view and every fragment of glitter on his face sparkles like its own individual disco ball. He tries to say something to me but I'm ragdoll dragged from our plinth into the cluster of bodies below, I barely catch myself, before I follow the trail of my arm to my hand to the interlaced fingers of Axel, still wearing a shirt, smiling manically as we jump and dance and the drag queens flank us, towering almost two feet taller.

Fairy fingertips lacing with my own, they unlace and slide a pill in between my lips. I chase it with the sip of my water bottle. We dance for what feels like hours. Underwater dancing, celestial dancing, we dance on clouds, through quicksand, being bustled and jostled by men with chests like hot cross buns, necks that splay southwards to bowling balls, tree trunk legs. There is neon, always neon, and chaos and grinding and noise from the music and noise from the fog machine and from people shouting at drops and transition, so much noise that it was resolves to nothing. I feel hands on my neck guiding me, hands on my chest worshiping me. Everything comes into my vision dazzling and zoomed in. Pores up close like craters, arm hairs stand tall, looking like a wheat field. 4K revelry.

"I needed this!" I scream in the direction of Axel's face. My armpits are damp from dancing and my skin feels like oil.

"Honey, we all did! And it's only the beginning of an amazing weekend!"

I break away from the crush, step off a dance floor that the pill and booze have turned into a turntable. My bladder sings. My top sways like a fox tail, threaded between belt loops behind me, as I move towards the bathrooms, the faint scent of piss and sanitiser growing more intense with every step closer. The crowd thins the further away from the bar and pit I get, and I smile toothy *Heys* at a couple of guys I recognise from around, but that doesn't stop me being shoved by a handsome blur of black leather and curls. Stumbling into the toilets, no fight in me as I continue this buoyant ascent, I check my phone as I approach up to a urinal. It's 12.28 AM and no messages from anyone, except a couple of despos on the app. I sigh, sliding the phone into my back pocket, unzipping myself out for a piss and leaning my head on the wall.

To my left, a Disney prince is a Gaussian blur. A little over my height, but that could be the thick soles of his sneakers. He has a buzzcut fade and hairy forearms, skin like kiln-fired clay. Knives for eyes, glistening wet knives, Japanese steel, boring into my own now, stood at the urinal, as twin streams of piss hit the back of the chrome and something German and bassy bears down on us. Dictionary definition of *shit-eating grin*, his teeth spread big bad wolf, and he says, "Having a good night?"

"I am, yeah," And I am, yeah.

His bladder empties quicker than my own. He buttons up, turns to me. "Want to have some fun?"

The cubicle is tight, claustrophobic, but I'm drunk enough and seeing glitter and fairy lights bokeh-style through air that's riddled with sweat and piss, and my prince is fishing down the back of my jeans with wet fingers, and we pant into each other's mouths, swapping CO_2 as I heave his shaft from his fly and stroke, a small wet trail tacking between the web of my thumb and finger. Moments ago, we both enjoyed a line, inhaled off of my phone, which lies on top of the basin. He still has a small smudge of white on his nostril, over which I rub the pad of my thumb and lick it clean.

He pushes me around, shoves down the waist of his pants, mine too. My ass is bared to the moist warmth of the room, his humid mouth meeting my cheeks, a firm hand pressing me to bend at a right angle. The rapid shift has my eyes watering a little, has my stomach in a small tumult. I almost collide with the basin, unnoticed by Prince Forceful. My eyes cross as he presses his tongue into me, and my phone lights up like an echo, two phones, moments ago a black dun brick and now, illuminated.

It's almost 1AM and Andrew is texting me. I can see his message from the home screen: *Glad you shrugged off that funk and you're having fun!* Winky face. I smile gormless as I feel my prince quickly press into me with his shaft, toothy display melting into gummy wide openness, eyes scrunching shut with bliss. My body is occupied by chemicals and alcohol and the thickness of another person, who slicks and slides back and forth gaining momentum. I react with pants and grunts as the length of his dick keeps hitting my prostate, making me dizzy, worrying my bladder again. He spits out invective like phlegm and it hits me straight at the root of my lust. I'm keening against him, matching the rhythm of his thrusts and the beat of the music bleeding in through the cracks of the door and the hinges. I see boots underneath the stall next to us, two pairs in my double-vision haze, my head lolling with the force of his fucking and the pressure of his grip on my skull.

The electronic music bleeds into something primal, something new. It sounds like high pitched laughing, hyena shrieks, then punctuated by the rat-a-tat of some nostalgic child's toy. The whirr and buzz of something mechanic, the repetition of a balloon popping, the slap of his skin against my own, our shared breath, it overwhelms me. I'm capsizing into climax. His fingers press into my hips, gripping hard enough to turn pink skin blue. I sink beneath the surf of the chems, under sex and lust, find myself losing purchase on the sound, it's intangible and grows more incomprehensible with every nudge to my spot, with every bite mark he leaves on my back.

Then, through the chaos, comprehension: screams. Gunshots.

I catch another glimpse of my phone.

1.06 AM.

Gunfire hitting the flimsy walls around us.

I feel him shoot inside me and it sets me off too and

I'm pulling out of the guy in the flat on Black Prince Road.

I am, in my own estimation, of a certain calibre, and London is the smallest big city I know, and so I manage to hold my nausea, push it down, until I'm on the street outside his flat, and I only throw up once I'm a few steps away from the door. My breakfast splatters mustard and chartreuse against the wall by the jitty next to the building, a couple of youths with cigarettes flinching and tutting at my vomit from across the way. I collapse next to my puddle of eggs and protein powder, can still see one of the fibre capsules I take undissolved, what a waste of money that is every month, and wipe the back of my hand over my mouth.

Eyes wide as pasta bowls, I sit, catching my breath, and enjoying the tactile sensation beneath me. The grit of pavement, the pebbledash pressing into my back. The lads are approaching, kids on safari, but I don't want to deal with anything right now.

"Y'alright, mate?" One asks.

"I'm fine." The words come out vibrato, which matches the steady tremor in my hands that I clock as soon as I stand and wipe my mouth once more with a gruff forearm. I look at the puke and then back at the strangers. "Sorry … about that." I pull my jacket together, hug myself, make moves towards the Needle. Again.

I take out my phone with intent to message Axel, trying to gain some composure, some mastery of my hands again.

20.50.

It stares me down in the corner of the screen as I type. As does his partner in crime on the home screen, *Jul 3*, smiling plainly in my face like a bully glaring down at his victim on the floor. I clench my hand hard, feeling the contours of my phone press into my skin, an ache beginning. My nose piggish, my brow furrowed hard like creased sand, I feel something bubbling from my stomach again, but it feels less like bile, something more nuclear.

I pound out the message. *Meet me at The Volunteer. Don't tell the guys.*

Then, in its wake: *Please.*

I haven't looked up in a minute and I've autopiloted my way to a corner in Little Portugal. I look behind me and see the handsome model in front of the coffee shop. Had I been out the house a half-minute later, we would be colliding a street over. The men are the same outside on the terrace. Familiar faces that would've gone unnoticed any other evening now haunt me third time around. People I had ignored – a lady with her pushchair; a straight couple leaving the supermarket on

44

the corner; tourists with luggage larger than themselves trying to cram onto a number 59 - they come into full focus like the images hidden within magic pictures, haloed by vignettes. And those faces look back at me, my greasy mouth that I keep wiping red raw to rid myself of the acerbic remnants of stomach acid and protein powder. They looked at me with curiosity, magnified disdain, I conjure whispers as I make a move towards the pub halfway between here and Elephant.

My phone vibrates in my hand. I pull it out, to check Axel's ETA.

See you in five. Thumbs up.

Axel finds me at the bar after 9PM, looking like I'm going up for the part of Junkie Number 2. Knee tapping away like I'm running a spinning wheel, my phone rests by my Tito's rocks, squeeze of lime, the coaster soaked with condensation. He drops his satchel, takes off his shades, flops into the banquette next to me. He looks harassed, his face blotted with brushstrokes of stress, ennui, crow's feet I hadn't clocked yesterday, or tonight, or two days ago, whenever it was or will be.

"What's up?" He says, leaning over to plant a peck on my cheek. I sniff and look at him. On any given day, his default is a devious squint like a fox, and he smirks like he knows something about you. These wide eyes now and the slight parting of his lips, the bullet hole of black I can see leading into my mouth, are new to me.

"I feel like I'm going insane." It comes out minutely, words thick with mucus. I can hear the bubble in my throat. He looks at me like shattered glass, a most sincere look, and I have to stop myself from breaking down right there, from baby crying, and falling headfirst into his lap. I sniff again, wiping my eyes with both hands, the bottom waterlines descending grotesque for a stretch before tensing back up.

"What's happened? Is it Nico?" His hand on my lap, the other on my shoulder.

"No, it's not Nico. I just think I'm having, like, a psychotic break or something."

"What make you say that?"

The bartender comes over. I don't look at him, but I see him assessing me, this. Axel gestures at my glass, says, "Two more of whatever that was." Looks back at me.

I sigh. "I think," A swallow. "I don't know. I think, like, I think that I've lived this day over." My face falls, I can feel it. "Like, I'm repeating it."

Axel doesn't speak, just looks at me as I try to communicate with all my might how real this feels, and how unable I feel to deal with it. There's a beat, and another, and then his eyebrow raises and he pulls back a little, like he's trying to get bigger scope, like he thinks the crazy is contagious, and I sink, I sag.

"I know this is ridiculous and it's out of some shitty streaming series, but I have done this before. July 3rd."

"Of course you have. It happens every year." Of course he went for levity.

"Axel."

"What do you mean, Bear?" And the fact that he says my name carries weight, added to the kilos I feel pressing on my shoulders.

"I have done this day before. I'm not kidding. July 3rd, day before Pride. I've been here, done this."

"Been … at The Volunteer?"

"No, not The Volunteer!" I whisper-shout. I look around a little. "This is new. But, like, just now, I was at a hook up and—"

He scrunches his brow. "You went to a hook up before pre-drinks?"

"Yeah, but the point is—"

"Are you on G?"

The question feels like a slap, like a deluge of cold water. The drinks are placed before us and I expect him to sip but he just moves his fingertips to hold the glass.

"No, Axel, I'm not high. He wasn't high and horny." Press lips, exhale through the nose. "It was a normal hook up. But it wasn't the first time I've woken up there." That fucking eyebrow again. "Not like that. I mean, I keep going through the day and then it gets to the end and it …" I drift off into the middle distance, can feel myself growing heavy with dread, with the ricochets of bullets in my ears, the mushroom cloud of fire and debris spilling out of the club.

47

"… Repeats?" Axel coaches me, but I barely hear it.

"The bomb."

Whirlpool eyes from him now. "*Bomb*?"

"I think? Or a shooting. Or something. At Glitch last night." I shake my head. "Tonight, I mean." Axel looks frustrated but I plough on. I'm chatty as a toddler now, my energy renewed. The knee is off again. "Tonight. I go to Jared's. Then we all go Glitch. And around one AM, something happens." Swallow. "Axel, something bad happens, and it's happened twice, and I think it's going to happen again."

"What happens exactly, Bear?"

"I don't know, but it's bad and fucking brutal and I know this sounds batshit—"

He slouches back, takes another drink. "At least you know."

"Fuck off, I know. I can hear myself."

"This is your job. Your career." He sees me looking to dismiss his comment. "No, Bear, it is. You were just telling me how work is drying up and it's stressing you out. You just got back from Vienna a few days ago and you're exhausted." A pointed sip of his vodka. "You're not in your twenties anymore, Bear."

"Yeah, I'm fucking reminded of it every day. This isn't that."

"No, Bear, this is." I see red spots beginning to dapple over his cheeks and nose, across pale skin like milk tainted by ink. "I'm not going to sit here and entertain this. You pulled me downstairs from Jared's for *this?*" Finishes his drink. "I don't know what this is but look at the timing. Your job, Pride, Nico–"

"This has fuck all to do with Nico."

"You've started drinking more since you guys broke up. I mean, the fucking around, the drugs?"

"*You're* lecturing *me* on chems? I'm sorry, what's German for hypocrite?"

"*Fotze.* Look it up."

I catch the eye of one of the staff, wave my hand in the air for the bill. I sniff, rub my eyes hard. "You know what? I thought you'd be the one to understand. Axel Blaschko, creative, producer, general *weirdo* who doesn't flinch at the shit he sees in Berghain, but no, something a bit fucking left field from his friend and he throws down ex-boyfriend issues with a side of addiction fake news. Fucking hell." I almost smash my smart watch, almost break my wrist on my card machine the bartender has quietly brought over. He's gone before the receipt can even print, fleeing the hysterical man in the burgundy suit and the leather queen with a badgery face. "Fuck off back to Jared's then, and have fun with all the guys!" I head for the door.

Axel's parting shot: "Nico won't take you back, Bear!"

Over my shoulder, which is bunched with tension and frustration, "And Andrew won't fuck you!" And I'm out the door.

My phone is out of my pocket as soon as I feel fresh air.

"Police, fire, or ambulance?"

"Police." My voice is shaking but I manage to get a grip. I stomp and feel the soles of my McQueen sneakers squeal with the force I put into every step. I can feel my heart running like an idling motor, like I just snorted some coke with caffeine. There's a slight whine in my ears, it reminds me of tuning my violin.

"This is the Metropolitan police—"

"There's going to be an attack." I cut him off before his spiel can get going. I freeze, sandwiched between two doorways, as I speak. "A bomb. A shooting."

"OK, sir. Is it a bomb or a shooting?"

"It's both." I scrunch my eyes up momentarily. "I mean, it was a bomb. But then it was a shooting."

"Sir, you aren't making any sense."

"Glitch nightclub. At one AM. There was an attack."

"There *was?*"

Fuck my life. Through gritted teeth: "There *will be* an attack. A shooting. We need the police there. Elephant and Castle, Glitch nightclub."

I wander down a residential road, past a pub on the corner, spot lit every few steps by a streetlamp. Over some yards to my right, as I make my way down the crescent, a group of youths sit outside a play area with BMX scattered at their feet.

From the phone: "Sir, have you been drinking?"

I pause and bring my phone to my face, glaring at it. Feeling like I've been sparked in between the eyes. His tinny voice comes out of the speaker minutely, repeating the line again, but I feel a heat blanketing my hackles. His voice turns elastic and shrill as I zone out, little beestings of irritation prickling my cheeks. The heat washes over into chill and I slowly bring the phone back to my ear.

"No, I haven't been drinking." I'm surprisingly calm. "Are you taking me seriously? People will die if we don't do something."

"Sir, are you involved in this at all?"

"No!" I see a couple of the lads turn to look at me from across the road. "I'm not, I just–"

"May I ask how have you come across this information?"

I stumble as I try to come up with the least insane sounding reply. Try to workshop an answer in the space of a millisecond. Responder, however, beats me to the punch.

"Sir, this number is for legitimate serious calls only."

A boxing glove to the gut. "This is fucking–" I hang up, my arm dropping wanly to my side. *Ridiculous*, I finish in my head.

South London is the centre of the universe. What it lacks in poor transport links, what people call poor transport links but with which I've never had an issue, not everyone needs a tube station, the Thameslink being the secret life hack of the London commute, but what it lacks its supposed disconnect to the rest of the city, it makes up for which the culture and the vibrancy and the diversity and the talent. Also, it's fucking gay. Transplanting from Fleetwood at the age of twenty-two, with a credit card and a heap of student debt, I ended up picking the cheapest place to live at the time, and cheap here is a relative term, welcome to London, and so Streatham Hill became home, just a ten-minute bus, an ambitious ten minutes, from Clapham. Before gentrification bleached over the city in big brushstrokes, I settled into a bedroom above an Ethiopian cafe, long before the Aussies and Kiwis came south with their flat whites and Violet Crumbles, and upgraded over the next decade from there.

I don't think any stretch of the city has seen me looking quite as panic-riddled as my home address right now. Moments out of the Uber, I feel the salt-dappled ribbons on my skin from the tears squeezed out from stress over the last half-hour, the way I feel like I'm wearing my body, riding my bones, foreigner in my own flesh. Exhaustion holds a blade above me as the clock strikes 9.30 PM. Key card in hand, I make it through the gates of my building and through my front door and the only noise I hear is blood pumping thickly in my ears and static in my head. I spent the entire drive home searching the web for answers, knowing it was futile, fruitless. My ads immediately started bartering with me for copies of *Groundhog Day*, sci-fi novels, books on science I can't wrap my ahead around. I felt the power drain from me with each link I pressed, each thread I went down on message boards, realisation slowly filling in the gaps like spilled paint that I was, objectively, a lunatic.

I feel gross, can't explain it, feel like I need to remove the clothes I'm wearing, burn them, jump in the shower and exfoliate everywhere I can reach until I feel fresh. I start to undress in the hallway, kick off my sneakers, slough off suit and shirt. I snatch them like popcorn and launch them into the utility, making tracks to my bedroom, in socks and briefs, and find myself moments later under scalding jets in the en-suite. I keep tapping the notch on the heat, nudge nudge to reach infernal temps, until I see my forearms and chest turning salmon pink. My teeth acting like pestle and mortar, I wash, scrub, drag nails across my skin until my triceps are traced with lines, my thighs too, and then, a swift scoop around the dial and brace for frozen impact: lashings of icy water hit me with thunderous effect, my breath hitching. An old fat loss wives tale that I can't let go of, it's doing double duty today, adding to the procedure I'm drafting on the fly to help me deal with July 3rd.

Five to ten, and I sit in sweatpants and t-shirt in my kitchen, the balcony doors to my right open and framing miles and miles of south London's circuit-board beauty. In one hand, a mug of fruit tea; the other holds my phone, through which I flip in search of a name I can latch on to. *Rendezdude* buzzes, letchy message with blue wording, but I decline to delve further. I go through the group chats, I open and close every conversation with Jared, Andrew, Robbie, actively ignoring the radio silence from Axel.

I hover over Nico's name in the archived folder. I swat away another notification from *PigDeviant* with an eye roll. My thumbnail finds its way in between my front teeth and I press down, not puncturing. I swipe the air just above his name, minutely, until my vision loses focus and I find myself sinking into the mud of six months ago. I can see Nico outside the bar in Clapham, dappled blue with strobes and orange with the heat lamps affecting nothing in the smoking area. He wears the coat I bought him for Christmas, a long grey camel number, and the most unattractive face I have seen him sport all night. They are well deep back in the bar, the window is painted black, but through the vignette of memory, I see silhouettes of all of our friends, my friends really, curtain twitching as Nico and I continue our argument, which started four minutes ago on the sofas by the mezzanine.

"Bear, you're drunk." He doesn't even look at me.

"No, no, carry on, why don't you carry on what you said in there?" I said drunkenly.

He takes out a pack of cigarettes, sparks up and exhales as I stand there, level with his chest, swaying a little and trying to focus on him, to bring the two blurs of him in my vision into harmony.

"This isn't an argument we need to be having now."

The smoke from his cigarette is misting my eyes up. I'm weeping a little as a crush of frustration which started in my base of my neck presses forward until it reaches for the front of my skull. I'm losing grip on the thread of the evening, ten minutes ago, we were all laughing with drinks scattered across the table like jewels, barbs and jibes being launched back and forth as some pop song blanketed the room, a drag queen getting her life on the glittery stage, but now, like a silk ribbon, I can't find purchase on the evening. A harmless comment from my mouth prompted a reaction in Nico I've never seen before, and back and forth until conversation around the group turned quiet and our own voices grew louder and Nico is reaching for his coat and not looking at me, and mumbles something under his breath, and my hazy, inebriated mind inflates it tenfold until I'm storming after him and here we are, under the heat lamp outside in January frost, my only outerwear the thick layer of alcohol in my body, pointing a lazy finger at my boyfriend.

Soon to be ex, tick tock, the argument will be over in less than three minutes, and he'll be out of the flat in two days. This same flat, the one in which I sit now, with tea warming me from the inside, bringing me back to myself, my cheeks puffy and red with nostalgia, almost blotting out my vision.

I move to my desk, grab a pen and the nearest sheaf of paper I see. My phone buzzes, I see another hook up request, another hand reaching out in the darkness. I flip the phone over, put pen to paper.

> *9PM – 11.30PM? Drinks at Jared's*
> *walk down to*
> *11.30PM Glitch*
> *circa 1AM. Incident?*

Lines splay and branch from each of these notations as I jot more detail, scratching my stubble as I think and work. Time stretches on. I close my eyes and play back the two days just gone, the July 3rds through which I've already lived, and try to focus on every motion I went through. Faces, people, names, locations, mapping repeated instances. If I'm honest with myself, have to be, I only really care about midnight onwards. My thumbnail returns home to my teeth again, little serrated pickets being carved minutely on my incisor.

"Where does it all begin?" I say, thinking out loud, swirling in the margin. My phone chirrups beside me, nudging itself around a little. Twice. Three times. I rub a knuckle over the bridge of my nose, pick it up.

HUNGarian writes:
You free?
Looking now?

Top/bottom?

I roll my eyes, slide open the messages on reflex, browse through the profile. Faceless with a muscular body, he is a few hundred feet away, I'm guessing one of the estates between here and Balham. The profile is bare bones, just stats and nothing else, just tells me he's my age and a little shorter than me.

Not interested, sorry, I reply. It's almost eleven o'clock. I yawn and move into the bedroom, pristine from the cleaner who came this morning, save for today's outfit thrown about like chunky confetti. I sit on the bed as another message comes through.

Fuck you then. His profile disappears. Blocked.

"Hey Axel, I'm sorry about earlier. Look, I don't want things to be awkward, so please can we just write it off and enjoy the weekend? I'm burnt out, like you said, and I just want a fun night out to take my mind off everything. I'm just about to hear to Glitch?"

I stand in the hallway, coat on, poised to bounce. My thumb stays holding down the record button for my audio note. He hasn't replied to the last few texts I sent, all variations of damage control. I let it go on for a few more seconds, erring between sending and deleting, before, fuck it. Deleted. Let's retry in a minute.

The group chat is a twitter, surprisingly so if you didn't know them since they're all in the same apartment. Axel markedly silent, Andrew already sniffing around, dropping a line directly at-ing me, *Why's the Bear in hibernation?* They communicate the POA, plans I think I know already. Jared mentions a couple of friends coming who were at pre-drinks. Goosebumps and a blossom of ice somewhere between my liver and stomach.

I write, *Who you thinking?*
Robbie and our friend Fred.

I deadpan the phone. "Fucking 'Fred'? That's how we're pronouncing 'Fred' these days?" I say aloud to no one.

A calendar invite alerts, announces itself on my phone, forwarded from Andrew, ever the planner. We're all CC'ed. Tickets for Glitch tonight, in just under an hour. It feels like a knife is being wriggled around my guts, a blade that has spent the last few hours in liquid nitrogen. Keys in hand, half out the door, I slam the door shut again, the noise flat and expansive, and I sink to one knee. I scrunch my eyes shut, flinching at the sounds of gunfire, the orange blossom of fire, the clogging, choking sensation of being fucked to dissatisfaction. I dropped my phone, it lays beside me now, and my breathing comes in shallow and rapid. I can't catch the oxygen fast enough, falling to my right and hitting the wall. A small tap to the back of my head adds a flash of white-yellow in the foreground, dizziness dogpiles on top of my weak knees and overworked lungs.

There's a folded sheet of paper in the breast pocket of my coat. My annotations from earlier, and they feel as useful as fuck all, sugar paper in a leather bomber graffitied with worthless scratch. I know nothing, except a time and a place, and I don't understand why me, what happens if I get to tomorrow, how I get to Saturday. There's a looming, Lovecraftian bleat, like bad weather sirens, stalking around the perimeter of my ears, and the louder the pitch grows, the inepter I feel, can feel my pointlessness coat my skin slick in tandem with the sweat from my stress.

A time and a place.

I open my mouth wide, swallow great goldfish breaths, allow myself to slink down so I'm horizontal on the parquet before the door. Focus on relaxing, on breathing deep, taking in, and breathing out just as long. I keep thinking about it, the time and the place, and I settle. I open my eyes, blinking at the dazzling LEDs above, sight blotching with artefacts.

Glitch. 1AM.

At times, it feels like the smallest city in the world. You can't go five feet without running into some three degrees off connection. You can nod your head at most guys in a mile radius of Soho, Vauxhall, even up-and-coming Brixton, and you'll likely get one back. A few weeks ago, found myself outside some station West, Hounslow or somewhere I had no business being if it wasn't for god father duties, and me and this Channel 5 Zac Efron type nod at one another crossing by the station. Never seen him before, just admiring the view, but he splits a grin and nods back, cushioned with a *hey*. We stop, turns out we were both just being polite, thought we knew one another's face. That turned into an enjoyable interlude en route to see friends. Sorry, Lucie, tube was a nightmare.

Point is, you likely know all the gays already, or if you don't, someone you know does. Which is how I skipped the queue by myself and weaselled my way first class into the club. Thank you, Michael. All it took was a wink and a twenty.

The rooms spill out before me and I realise this is the first time I'm seeing the inside of the club sober. There are still fragments of gem tones being thrown around the room by the lighting rigs above the DJ booth, and fog and sweat and a million different colognes priced at varying degrees along the economic spectrum mist the air, but it's a cattle market in the pit of the dance floor below. I still wear my shirt and jacket, even though the air is thick with heat, as I delicately elbow my way across the room in search of any of the guys.

My vision blurs a little with each thud from the speakers, the squeal of techno, but I finally spot the heads of Andrew and Axel as they trot up the stairs towards the bar. It takes me a minute to reach them, placing a hand on Axel's forearm just as he's about to be served. He turns, a moment of irritation stretched on his face. I recoil a little. Patent leather black Chelseas from Steve Madden, black leather jacket from All Saints, smug sardonic look, model's own. I see Andrew is looking at me with hesitation, and then Axel's mouth folds itself into the left dimple at the corner of his lips.

"Axel has been known to exaggerate." Toy time over.

"Bear, it sounds like you've been having a rough time," Andrew offers, his face genuinely a little concerned.

"Yeah, and like you've gone nuts."

I fix a grin to my face. "I've no idea what you're on about."

Axel cocks his head. "Our conversation at The Volunteer?"

"Oh, that? I was just being dramatic, embellishing a little. Adding a little creative flair."

"There's nothing creative about you."

"I'm a violinist and compose scores. There is everything creative about me."

Axel rolls his eyes and turns to the bar, ordering *two* drinks. I roll my own at the math.

"Look," says Andrew, pulling me a few feet from the counter. "We're … worried about you. Those things you said to Axel?"

I turn to shrug it off, to see Jared approaching us. He spots me and his face goes from elated to bored. It's bizarre that I can almost see the strings supporting his smile snap. His gait slows but there wasn't much space between us all to begin with.

"You shouldn't be here, and you shouldn't be drinking."

"Hi to you too, Jared."

"We don't think it would be appropriate."

My eyes widen. "What?"

Axel arrives with drinks for him and Andrew. "We aren't being dicks. You were talking crazy talk earlier, and we don't think it would be responsible to co-sign that by letting you get shitfaced this weekend."

"But I could just leave now and get shitfaced?"

"That wouldn't be on us. It's also proper bad form to go for a fuck instead of coming to a house party thrown by your *friend*." Jared looks around to Axel and Andrew for agreement, which they offer in spades with intent nods.

"So you're saying ... I can't sit with you?"

Andrew puts a hand on my bicep. "Mate, go home. Take the weekend off. Head to Brighton or something."

"Get yourself together."

"Sort yourself out."

They're all staring at me, bugging me out with three pairs of feline eyes glowing sapphire, ruby, amethyst. My mouth is half open, crooked smile as I realise they're serious, realise I'm not going to get through to them. Plan B, trying to see if my vanity muscles hold any weight and drag them all out kicking and screaming, seems like a delusion now. Vanishes like candyfloss in water as the pain of distrust digs talons into my skin, my heart. As I stand, I think of the spiel that coats my tongue, the pleas to not follow the path that leads of agony, to death, to chaos. I look everywhere, to the floor, back and forth, and huff, cough.

"Um, wow." I take a half step, reverse. Look at all three of them. I nod.

I'm going to get annihilated.

I have no idea who these people are. Someone says they recognise me from Instagram and I have a shot poured down my throat. Black and sticky. I dribble a little ink stain on my shirt, and the two sisters are laughing, and there's a guy with a solid grip on my forearm, and there's one I like the look of, tall and Grecian, a slice of Mykonos about him. We bustle, it's the only word, from smoking area to bar to dance floor, and this group, these people who picked me up from drowning myself in Fresher's Week shots, chasing with expensive vodka, they're warm and fluffy people, not barbed wire boys like Axel or Jared or any of the guys I see daily who happily brunch with you, swing around poles and drag queens and neck Buck's Fizz but the second the status quo is interrupted, you're queried, quarantined, exiled in increments with fewer invites. I'm holding on to my Spartan, with terracotta skin and grotto eyes, and laughing, and they all have names I've forgotten, remembered, mashed together like clay, and slurred out. Someone has gear, I think, and 300 leans over and asks if I want a key.

Cut to not-so-straight Spartan, should've know from the boat shoes, rolled up cuffs, the animal print shirt, pushing me against the wall in a bathroom cubicle. There's something playing that wouldn't be amiss in

Ibiza, or on Love Island, and I laugh into the crook of his neck, a bubbly giggle that rankles 300. I hear him knead his back and mumble something like *fucking camp* as he fishes in the front of my crotch, grabs me hard, and begins to jerk. I mirror him, finding him lacking but work with his package, caressing him until his pointed comments turn into mewls and breathing sighs. My head hits the back of the wall and a vibrations thrums through me as my jeans ride lower and my dick touches the sticky cool air of the bathroom and his sweaty smell mixed with body spray reaches my nose.

My breath hitches as 300 brings me closer to climax, his hands rough, his technique sloppy and perfunctory, the coke seemingly doing nothing to impede my libido. The buzzing sensation continues down my body and I realise that my phone is vibrating in my breast pocket in time with the building, with the thrum of vibrations echoing around us. As my Spartan keeps gumming at my throat, clutching my ass cheeks hard, as I rock him towards his own orgasm, I reach for my phone and see the display.

AXEL calling.

I almost cancel the call, but deviant excitement prompts me to answer, enjoy the conversation as 300 jerks me to completion.

"What?" I hear my voice, barely, and it's as thick and viscous as treacle. It hits me how much I've drank. My Spartan gives me a cursory look, rolls his eyes, and I swear he shifts gears, tries harder, brings more of himself into the space with us to make this feel better.

"Bear!" It's noisy, only a few rooms over, but he's drowning in shouts and cries, and what I think is the steady hiss of a fog machine. "*BEAR*!"

"Axel?" My voice hitched as 300 sinks down and takes me, a shock, into his mouth.

"They're killing us!" There's a xylophone trill, low, and thuds and bangs, and I'm not sure if it's me shuffling as my knees buckle or coming for the earpiece. I feel cold suddenly, wading through the sod of memory, and I'm riding his mouth. My phone is loose in my grip. I hear the door to the toilets slam open, followed by a couple of popcorn blasts.

"What?" I'm gagging on a little bit of bile that has made its way up from my belly. I'm treading water but it's quicksand. Axel's voice is wave hitting the surf, crashing against rocks, seashell in my ear. I try to push 300 away but I'm listless.

Fewer Christmas cracker blasts in the bathroom and I hear a scuffle from behind the other side of the door. Hear a husky strained voice scream, "You *cunt*!" and then a wet, heavy plop like a bath bomb being dropped.

"You were right!" Snap, crackle, and pop, and I'm brought back into the club. Glitch. Gunfire. The tumult and tempest of the attack, the shriek and wail of voices, the bellow of men as bullets lance their skin, my mind runs away with me, and I lose the thread of it all, and unravel into orgasm. Axel's voice fades into a high pitch like a modem, like magnetism.

And I'm in his bed again.

Black Prince Road.

Balls deep in a guy whose name escapes me.

I feel rough. Might give drinks tonight a miss. Straight into the group chat.

Inside the flat, just a solo reply from Andrew, I fall face first, still dressed, onto my bed, my head hitting the pillow, and I scream. A great yell of noise, incomprehensible, into the fabric. It feels like it stretches on for hours but realistically, it's over in less than ten seconds. I roll onto my side, stare out of the window, the south of the city spread like glitter. Stare until my eyes part ways, the glitter gets less sharp and my vision blurs. I press a button by my bedside table and the room is lit only by the mustard lights from other flats opposite on the quad.

My phone has found its way onto the pillow before me, don't remember putting it there, and I reach for it. Ignoring the wall of notifications, I find my contacts list, hover over a name. I call, put it on speaker, no energy to hold it to my ear.

After an age, "Hello son. Everything alright?"

I swallow. "Hey Dad." Too much vibrato, I clock. "I'm good, thanks. How're you?"

"We're alright here. Your mother is at work still, and I'm just playing Bejewlled before bed." His accent, Lancashire thick like a wooden fleece.

"That's nice," and I feel my face getting hot as tears arrive at my waterline and a couple have the temerity to spill over. "What you had for tea?" I just want to bask in his voice, in the normalcy of the moment. A phone call back home, miles and leagues away from the mind-churning, spit-in-your-face lunacy of this ceaseless circuit.

"Just a curry. Not too spicy, you know how delicate she can be. Found a great recipe in your grandmother's cookbook, and there was a decent catch the other day. You remember your mate Charlie's dad? Hooked us up with a great deal on some cod."

"That's good, I ain't spoke to Charlie in ages." I hear some of Fleetwood coating my tongue again, and cringe, but smile too.

"Everything OK down there? You sound rough."

I sniff, pointedly away from the phone, and gather myself as best I can. "Yeah, yeah, was just calling to say hey. I ain't phoned in ages, and I think I'll be a bit too drunk to call over the weekend."

"Well, don't be silly with the drink. You don't want to turn out like your Uncle Paul."

"I can handle my ale, Dad."

"I'm sure you can." And his voice is a wink. I roll my eyes and then myself out of bed. I stretch around the uncomfortable creases in my clothes, rub my eyes. I haven't napped but I can't count how long it felt like I was on that bed. "Not out tonight?" He asks.

"I'm not sure yet," I reply, padding into the kitchen. I see the clock: 10.45PM. "I just have a lot on, not sure if tonight is a good idea."

"And why's that?"

"I just," I don't never know where the sentence is going. "I have a lot on my plate right now. There's a … score that I feel like I'm going round and round in circles with. Running into a lot of obstacles." I smile wryly at myself.

"I can't help you with your music, I'm afraid. That was never my wheelhouse." He pauses, I hear him take a sip of something. Can imagine him seated on the patio in the back garden back in Fleetwood, laptop on his thighs, Santana playing in the background. "Just keep the end in sight and persevere, son."

"I just keep on going back to square one and no matter how many times I try…"

"You know what the definition of insanity is."

"No, I know," and I do, but only when he says it do I feel the notion taking root in me. I yawn. "I'm just burnt out from it all."

"I'm sorry to hear that. Maybe a night out with friends is what you need to take your mind off it?"

He says *friends*, and the men in my life rush express service to the fore. I slink to the floor, my back against the wall, my hand holding the phone beginning to tremor, as Andrew's bald head, sun-splotched face comes into view, and with it, the warmth of his embrace. I see Jared, high forehead, beak of a nose, and feel the lacing of his fingers on a dance floor. Even Axel, catty and vindictive fresh as a papercut, but the sight of him folding my clothes in this very room the night after Nico and I split. It's not bearable, the pain that pushes from being the eyes and around the heart and tries to invade every crevice in me. I can hear Axel's voice, I conjure images of Jared felled, Andrew struck down, things I haven't even seen but can clearly picture, cyclical. The bodies of people I don't even know, too, bright fluorescent paintings like a horror movie, like a disaster film, a looping macabre vignette. It threatens to push me through the floor, this weighted despair of that what hasn't happened yet, the pre-grief, and yet has happened more than once already.

I barely realise my Dad is still talking. I zone back into his words. "Bear, son, are you OK?"

I take a sweeping gulping breath, hear the shudder of air coming in. Count to five. "Yeah, Dad, you're right. Maybe I'll head out tonight. I just need to get ready."

We swap *I love yous* and hang up.

I need to get changed.

Clock strikes 11.30PM when I sidle up next to the boys in the queue for Glitch. I saw a swathe of familiar faces as I strode past and beelined for my place next to

Andrew. Their faces spread into warm, crafty smiles, Andrew's being the most sincere.

"Look at her!" Andrew says as he hugs me. He sizes me up. "She brought out the Loubs."

I faux blush, camp it up. "These old things?"

"And those pants are *painted* on." Robbie snipes playfully over Axel's shoulder.

"Fuck *off*," I say. I move to Jared, kissing him on the cheeks as I whisper an apology into his ear. *Bad form, hope you didn't miss me*. Axel salutes me and offers me a can of pre-mixed cocktail discretely. I brush it off delicately.

Jared looks as me queerly. "Bear Griffin, not drinking?"

I wink at him. "Let's see how the night goes."

We make it into Glitch, my body thrumming with coiled apprehension. I look like I'm on something, my eyes scatty, my hands loose cannons as I try to still them in my jacket pockets, but they flit like magpies over to Andrew's shoulder, Jared's arm, Axel's wrist. The guys are enough into their cups that they aren't stressing with how tactile I am. I keep glancing at my watch, trying not to look like I'd rather be anywhere but here.

I've never felt proper claustrophobic before but the crush of the crowds as we move from the box office to the loos to the bar to the dance floor is cloying. Maybe because I'm sober, I declined the coke offered in the toilets, but the throng, the seemingly ceaseless encroach of bodies all around has me dizzy. I tap out. Behind me

71

I can barely hear cries from a couple of them, see Robbie taking his top off finally, before I'm up a couple of steps from the pit and push my way to the smoking area.

I unthread my shirt from my belt strap, put it on as I wade through. The crowd begins to thin and I nod *hellos* to a few of the men I recognise. Once I'm between a cold place and a sweaty one, I take out my phone.

12.45PM.

The night has escaped me. After almost an hour of dancing and observation, albeit I should've done less of the former, my feet are swell and hurt as I make my way to the bathrooms, recalling gunfire as I was fucked to completion in a cubicle. The DJ, some generic Scanditerranean, picks up the pace, and the crowd in the adjacent room roars with delight and intoxication, and my heart plummets one floor in the shaft of my body as I wish I was enjoying the high of the night.

I pass the dark room, two Insta models, looking so serious as if it were their job to look so serious, leaving the fog of the room with their bum bags, giving me a leer. I barely acknowledge them as I press forward to the toilets. Spartan walks by and gives me a nod as he passes, which I parry with a furrowed brow, a shake of my head. He rolls his eyes, moving further on the hunt. Shouts and jibes are launched above me, around me, as I turn down a thin hallway which stinks like disinfectant and sewage.

I enter the gents, see a few guys hanging by the sinks as one of their friends finishes off at the urinal. This is one of the quieter toilets, I know from past experience, set far away from the dance floor and bars. Probably why Spartan had chosen it last night. I go to the urinal and take a leak, waiting for the guys to leave, pressing my head against the frame above. Their laughter and talk fades and I look over my shoulder to see I'm alone.

I tuck myself back in and check the time. 12.52PM. I crouch on the floor and look under the stalls, trying to find someone hiding? I don't know what I'm looking for, waiting for an incident to occur, would be even better if I could just prevent it. The floor is grotty and I feel a dampness press into my knees, into the palm of my supporting hand, sparing a couple brain cells to bristle at the state of my Dries pants. Rookie fucking mistake, Bear.

The toilets are empty. Were it not for the lack of a door at the entrance, out of which I can see the long hallway, thin as a matchbox on its side, leading to the main rooms, I would feel cocooned. I swirl around and look at myself in the sink, clutching the edge hard. I have no leads except a time and a place. My heart is picking up speed, rabbiting along as I examine my eyes in my reflection. I hear sounds of laughter coming nearer, and look to see Mr. 300 himself striding down with some muscular otter. Fingers looking like they're down the back of the lad's jeans, they're sucking face and barely notice me as I cross them to leave. I wince as I pick up the pace, my toes announcing their discomfort. I tread out of the hall and make moves towards the main room.

There are a couple of pops, loud enough to hear over the thrum of the music and hiss of the smoke machine. I feel them announce themselves staccato under my feet over the rhythm of the bass. Across the way, near the entrance to the main room, I see a man running towards the double doors. Dressed in rubber pants, combat boots, and a harness, he fumbles with the pull doors, turns on his heel to be greeted by a spray of bullets.

I flinch back, unable to see the shooter, but can't run. The toilets are behind me but all I can do it was the slow sluice of life leaving this man. A shadow approaches, covering him from the toes up like a sunset. His head lolls over to face me, and there's a glacial look in his pasta bowl wide eyes and I know he's gone, beyond all help, and I have given myself one job to do, but the soles of my shoes are anvils. The shadow of the shooter encroaches more. I can make out broad shoulder, height, and bulk that forces my hand.

I turn, tripping over my *fucking shoes*. I clamber to my feet with grime on my face, my hands, feeling like my nose is smashed in, and tread, as quickly as I can, to the toilets. I bolt into a cubicle, any cubicle. My face is hot with pain and my nose feels like a piece of clay smushed in the middle. I hear more pops in the distance, the music ceaseless, the screaming beginning.

Pants and groans come from a couple of cubicles over as I peep through the crack into the bathroom. I have a thin line of sight as a shadow comes closer, taking form. He steps into the bathroom, the yellow-purple lights too low to add specifics to the silhouette. I catch a slice of his face as he steps under one of the bulbs, but he's too distant for me to guess anything other than he's a tall, broad, white man.

He stops at the first door his left, squats, looks under. I watch as ice floods me, as I take the quietest step backwards onto the toilet bowl.

He shoots a few rounds through the first door. There's music playing somewhere but all I can hear is distant gunfire and my own minute breathing and the small splish-splash of his tread. I scrunch my eyes closed and then force them back open, force my hand to stop shaking as I steady myself against the hinges, carry on peeking through the crack.

The shooter passes to the second door, another half a magazine emptied.

I can barely breath. I've never seen guns before in real life. This is England, not the States. I wouldn't be nearly choking on the bile of terror were this man holding a knife, but he can get through this room in less than a minute if he wants.

To my right, the clamour of a toilet door opening.

The guys from earlier, Spartan and the otter.

I swerve to watch the shooter turn around to face them. It's difficult with only a slice of a few millimetres of see. I'm straining hard not to shake the cubicle in terror.

The moment stretches out for a lifetime. I swear I can see something almost physical passing before me, between the shooter and the men. A viscous understanding. I'm going dizzy as I try and still my breath, I'm cramping somewhere between my groin and neck. The shooter steps forward, raises the gun, and I can see more of his face now. I commit as much as I can to memory, trace my eyes through the crack in the door, in the dim light, through the static that threatens to cloud my vision pushed on my stress and panic and terror. I betray myself, my dick leading the charge, thinking, *he's almost handsome.*

From Spartan, "What the—"

Pop pop. And then a huff, a thud, meat falling to the floor.

A choke leaves my throat, unprovoked.

He turns to me, the shooter, and I fall back. I knock my tailbone on the toilet and I hear his footfalls. He shoots the door next to me to confetti, I can see the shadow underneath, and I watch his stance change as he fixes aim at the door to my cubicle.

There's a champagne pop from somewhere in the hallway, sounds like the slam of one of the doors to the main room. I hope silently that it isn't the sound of door meeting someone's skull. From beneath the bottom of the cubicle, the shooter's shadow shift. I think he's turning.

Two loud gunshots, I feel one of them hit the door less than a meter before me, and then the shooter's body slumps to the ground. Just meat, I can make out his ass, the sight of his lax hand loosening grip on the trigger of his rifle as each second passes

The moment of relief is short lived as the new player has entered the game. I'm torn between rushing to the crack to get a look at contestant number two, and staying perched on the bowl, hoping to continue sleuthing once I've been left alone. I rub at my eye, realising that I couldn't feel tears leaking.

I need to get a grip, seriously.

To a soundtrack of cacophony and chaos delicate steps coming from outside the cubicle, I lean forward towards the sliver of vision I have. My heart is calamitous in its speed, my skin distilled energy. I feel like I've got sunburn.

The shadow standing flinches. His hair bounces buoyantly, I see, as he flourishes around as a different beat crescendos. I see him brandish the gun towards the hallway.

He raises it, I interpret that much at least, saying quite plainly, "Are you fucking kidding me?" in a voice that echoes in my mind. Ripples like a punch through a glass pane even as the gunfire recommences and I'm sliding out of a guy's hole in an increasingly more familiar apartment on Black Prince Road. He falls forward, as usual, slumps as I pull back onto my haunches. I let out a ragged breath and stare into the middle distance, sweaty, the metallic taste of terror still fresh on my tongue and in my mouth. I shake my head, try to swat away the panic, the nausea.

He's saying something I don't hear and I gruffly turn to face him.

"What is your name?" I yawn roughly. I feel knots in my muscles and soreness around the eyes.

He giggles, writhing a little, a waif among silk sheets. "You often fuck men you don't know?"

"Never mind then," I say, making moves to leave.

He sits up and I can *feel* him pouting a little. "It's Riley."

"Riley." I roll it on my tongue as I pull on my pants. Press a heel of my hand into one eye to rub off the snooze.

"So you're–"

"–about to fuck off to Valhalla. Wrong. House party down the road, then Glitch." His phone rings. I make my way to the door, and say just loud enough for him to hear, "It's your boyfriend, you should get that."

"Hey Jared, you got a sketchpad?" I grab him by the arm as soon as I'm in the living room. Axel greets me with a smile and puts a shot in both of our hands. We four toast, I throw it behind me, the liquor falling onto the rug. Andrew grimaces down the acid and looks at me funnily.

"You OK?"

"Fabulous." To Jared, "Pencil? Paper?"

He sets me up on the kitchen counter, and I begin scratching together an approximation of the faces I last saw through a thin slice of door in a dimly lit toilets. The last guy is a bust, but player number one might be easier. I just need a reference, just need enough to go off of later. After a couple of minutes, small faces dotting the page, I'm not an artist, didn't even pass the creative module in first year, Axel sidles up.

"What you doodling?"

A smile and a wink. "It's a secret."

"You're being anti-social, man."

"Asocial."

"No, I meant anti-social."

I huff and sigh. Put down my pencil. "Sorry, you're right." I gesture back at the sketch. "It's just a guy I had a dream about, and I think I might've seen him out before. He was fit, I think."

"Analog. Retro." A long pause from Axel, who sips pointedly from his highball as he stares at me. Assessing. "You OK?"

"Yeah, just shattered. Eager to see the weekend."

"Calm down. Night hasn't even begun yet and you're wishing it away."

I scratch scratch scratch some more, adding detail until I'm quietly confident of my doodle. "Too right."

Feet feeling like sausage meat squeezed into matchboxes, we move into Glitch. The same anthem is blasting, an endless stream of electric noise tethered to a midi player, Hans or Sven or Caio sweating onto his decks. I don't take off my top this time, don't even pretend to be interested in the dance floor, the crystals of booze lining the deep-purple backlit bar. I know most of the bartenders but barely acknowledge them as I beeline past everyone to the toilets, to the corridor leading to the toilets.

I see where he came from, to the left of the double doors that spill into the hallway down to the bathrooms. There's a shorter passage that I know leads to the smoking area. I head down, a couple of men passing.

I stand there, watching, drawing looks from many potential lays that any other day I would've led into the dark room, with whom I would've ended up in carnal contortions among grease and sweat in a shadowy, dirty corner. Their faces shift Picasso in the strobes as I try my best to parse the shooter, the potential threat, from the masses.

My phone buzzes in my pocket. Snaps me to attention again. It's 12.30AM and Axel is messaging:

Wo bist du?

He only switches to German when he's high, and I saw him inhale a whole pixie stick of coke back at the apartment. I tap a brief reply, *Gone hunting*, and I push the door into the smoking area.

A wall of chill hits me as I step out. It's cool compared to the humidity inside. Fairy lights stretch between little wood cabins like an urban Skegness. Men are dotted around in harnesses and not, in rubber and lycra, with whorls of grey smoke misting around heads. Again, a few familiar faces, whose eyes needle me as soon as the door behind me closes. I scan them, a photo on my phone of a crude portrait, a handful of faces who could be any of them. Right height, right build, all looking menacing and violent, Glitch doesn't exactly attract a happy smiley crowd, and no one wants to look tapped.

There's a small bar outside, a kiosk really, selling basic drinks, and I grab myself a half of cider. I find a low wooden wall in front of one of the cabins and sit and watch, trying to look inconspicuous, very aware I'm the only person there fully clothed. A couple of the older gents slink by, leering. I return a blank look and their toothy smirks drop like dead birds. I count roughly twenty men outside, all clustered in cliques with one another, a couple of randoms idling around solo, mostly by the slightly ajar fire exit.

No one looks to be making moves to launch a strike against all the dancing queens inside. There's a couple coming and going at the door, but no suspicious-looking fellows, no one hefting a great bag with a gun painted on the side. No cello cases. I yawn, rolling out a knot in my back I didn't notice was there. My eyes feel heavier but I keep scoping out the area as subtly as I can, rebuffing anyone who comes near, *Hey there*, *Not interested, sorry*, recipient of catty glares and outright insults. Security comes into the yard, does a brief sweep, picks up a couple of glasses. Slams the fire exit shut.

It's banal to frustration, to the point where I see I've wasted almost half an hour in here. More texts from Axel, one from Andrew, and my cider is untouched, condensation spilling down the side. My skin feels grotty from the smoke and I feel antsy, ready to explode with annoyance, at myself, at the situation. I put down the half pint glass. I'm vibrating, poised, trying to not look like I'm shivering, I'm that shaky, looking like a tweaked meth head to a curious eye, not that any of these eyes are curious for more than two snips of conversation and five minutes in the dark room.

Piggish nose and high forehead. Don't know why I didn't clock him before. The victim, the glassy eyes from the corridor, sunset shadow taking over his body, splattered against the double doors leading to the main room, he's one of the idlers, milling around near the fire exit, now heading to move inside.

My phone buzzes again but stays in my pocket as I begin to follow. I look around, seeing if there's another face in the crowds that could fit the profile of the shadow in the bathroom, but I can't pin any one guy down. No one seems to be making moves towards the exit either. I swivel back to find my man, mister soon to be aerated with bullets, but he's gone inside. I pick up the pace.

I roll my ankle, the shoes too fucking gross, my pants tight and I stack it, falling through the doors. The man stands there, the vic, passing time watching me try and get up. My exhaustion catches up with me in that moment and I'm sluggish to move, motions like moving through Vaseline, and he just watches. My feet pound in my shoes. I bring myself to my palms and knees, watch as a couple more people move from outside to in, all shirtless, in leather, in gear, all staring down at me as I clamber back onto my feet.

None with weapons.

A cold stone falls somewhere from high in my chest to my belly.

A hand grasps my arm and I turn rapidly to see the security man. "Can't stand up straight, you're pissed," he says, leading me back out the way we came, back into the buttercup lighting and ghosts of smoked tobacco. I can feel my lifeless face, slapped with the cold meaty hand of fatigue, and I protest listlessly as I'm dragged towards the fire exit. I press my heels to the floor, am met with a pulse of hot pain lancing from toe to calf.

Through the narrow alley between the fire exit and the street, another bouncer joins us and despite my cries that I'm sober, that my shoes are making me unsteady of my feet, that there's something about to happen, something terrible and violent, something bloody and deadly, I am pushed out the back entrance, a slice of road between the main roundabout and some small business estate. "Don't try and get back in," one of them launches at me as the door slams shut. I begin to orient myself, try and find the entrance. It takes me a moment before my mind can focus and I limp towards the roundabout, to the queue again, thinking to push myself in front of anyone to get back in. I hope Mike is on the door still.

Halfway down the alley, I hear it begin. Shouts, cries, gunfire, the stampede of hundreds of drunk, high, disoriented men looking for the nearest exit, tripping over bodies and bottles, running headfirst into barrels down which bullets careen until finding nests in their flesh. I halt. *No no no no no no no no.*

With slaughter just a couple yards away from me, seeing the queue flee across the ring road, bellows and shouts and pleas coming from inside the building, I limp around to my left and push as hard as I can to the front. I pass a few of the shriekers and flanking them, I bug-eye stare as phones are held aloft and Stories are updated with live footage. Rather than flee any further, a lot of individuals have decided a few metres from the entrance of the club is safety enough. Incredulous, a manic smile adorns my face as I heave against the current, elbowing out the way cookie cutter men in leather and denim. I seem to be making no progress, actually feels like I'm moving backwards, the pain in my leg flaring like a battle cry. There's a surf of musk and men and it pushes me awkwardly onto my side as screams and shouts still spill out of the gaping mouth of the building. I feel steel toe caps clip me in the flank and as I try to right myself, to place feet on the ground, an errant kneecap hits my cheek bone and floors me as the heel of a boot ends up pinching my neck and

"Fuck off, Riley."

I step into Axel's apartment minutes later, yawning widely. Greeted by my friends.

"Axel, I need to borrow some sneakers."

I've been AWOL for about twenty minutes, I reckon. In straight jeans, vom, and a pair of AF1s, Andrew approaches me as I sit on the edge of the bed, tapping away on my phone. I look up. He stands before in the spare room, drink in hand, and fixes me with squinty eyes and a head tilt.

"What?"

"'What?'" He parrots back. I toss my phone next to me and lean back on my palms. He stands at ease, pointing at me with the hand holding the drink. "You've been weird all night."

"Give it a rest, I've been up thirty hours," I say. My eyes are itchy from the math I've just been doing on my phone, among other things. We're slowly approaching my thirty-first hour as we get ready to go out to Glitch. The Uber will arrive in eleven minutes. We will queue for fourteen minutes. Cloakroom for another four minutes. By midnight, we are in the venue properly and then, tick tock, forty-five minutes and change until not even all the king's horses, puncture kits in saddlebags, could help half the party gays in London tonight.

"You haven't slept since Wednesday night?"

A wan smile, all I'm capable of. "Beginning to feel like Friday won't end."

"What's up, Bear? Is it work?" He takes a seat next to me, and the sudden shift on the mattress is enough coaxing for me to fall back on the bed. He looks back at me over his shoulder. "I know you feel the need to hustle all the time. Is it worth it?"

"I'm reliving the same day over and over," I say to the ceiling.

"It can feel like that sometimes. I have days like that. Sometimes weeks, even."

"And everyone keeps dying and I'm not smart enough to figure it out."

"You're plenty smart, Bear. And creative. Don't exaggerate, though." He puts a hand on my leg, squeezes, and there's a flash, an electric reminder of something that was snubbed out almost a decade ago.

I speak through bandages of fatigue. "Yesterday was different. Something was different that the usual routine."

"In a good way?"

"Maybe? It still ended the same."

"Well, maybe it's something you want to focus on, since you're bringing it up. What was so different?"

And like red wine on the table linen, his words bleed through the haze, the exhaustion, and my eyes open slowly, taking in the bokeh beige of the room. I sit up.

"*I* did something differently."

"Like a new take on a piece of music?"

"Something like that?"

"Then next time you're in the studio, feeling like shit, like the whole day is going to shit: do something different. Unpredictable. Try something you wouldn't think would make sense."

And there's a twinkly smile crinkling the corners of my eyes. I shake my head and turn to him. "I *actually* love you," I say and pull him into a great hug.

"How much for a bottle of Grey Goose?" is a sentence I never through I would say in Glitch. I grew up in Yates's, in 'Spoons, enjoying a bit of tongue in a discrete corner with some girl my age from work before I admitted my penchant for dick. Nights dotted with Jagerbombs, vodka Red Bulls, and a platter of other specials, two for one on quad vods, we all know the drill. But the image I've embodied in the past decade in London has been refined and tailored to not include bottle service in the VIP area, like some junior apprentice blowing his EMA.

And yet.

My AMEX flies out of my card holder into the bartender-cum-escort's hand and within a couple of minutes, I'm carting around a Pyrex cooler bucket filled with half-melted ice and a seriously marked-up bottle of vodka. Coupled with the lack of effort in my attire, but God the shoes are comfy, no cramps, and I can move in the jeans, I cringe thinking about the look I'm currently *not* owning.

I just spent the last half an hour scoping out more of the talent, mentally crossing off likely candidates again and again. I'm growing bored of the same faces and couple of times, I feel as though I'm ready to drop off. Now with the vodka, I move through a couple of different doors, passing from the main dance floor to a smaller bar on the west side, the kind of place the older gents go to sit and drink after dancing. It's dressed up like Aladdin's harem, reams of fabric strung from the low ceiling to bring the drug-takers and the cohorts to Marrakesh via SW1. I lose the ice bucket on the counter in there, grabbing the bottle by the neck, and making waves to the toilets. My watch says it's almost 1AM.

I make my way into the bathroom. I follow an invisible string from my sternum to the back wall behind the bowl and slam the door shut. I pour out the vodka, barely even marrying my money leaving my credit card to the sight of the liquor quite literally splashing down the toilet. The bottle empties and I sit and compose a brief text, copy and paste it into three different chats. To Andrew, to Jared, to Axel.

Meet me at the cloakroom.

I sit, my lips feeling dry, my nose filling with stagnant piss. Eye on the crack, I steady my breathing, my hand firm around the bottle.

Enter Spartan and his boy. They fall into the same cubicle. The same ministrations begin seconds later.

I can't bear to look at my phone. I know a minute will feel like an hour, and I worry I will fall down the well of staring clear through my phone to the floor below and will miss my chance to act.

Pop pop goes the gun, splish splash of his feet as he moves into the bathroom. My masked murderer, carrying more than just a prop from Bugsy Malone, it looks like the Audi of assault weapons. I try not to look at the prone body behind him in the hall, try not to breath too loudly, too suddenly. I unlock the door, as slow as I can, so slowly I question if I'm moving at all. He begins his attack on the empty cubicles. Clockwork. 300 steps out, shielding twink. I never noticed that before, and my pulse relaxes for a beat as I process this glimpse of selflessness. I see the shooter at my twelve o'clock facing quarter to three.

The bottle makes contact within seconds of me moving out of the cubicle and swinging my arm towards his head. He wasn't expecting me, to my delight, and his attention is noticeably split. I hold the bottle like a rounders bat and my eyes flash open with a celebratory jump, the corners of my lips prematurely joyous, because

90

the gunman is faster than anticipated, and turns to counter my blow with his weapon. The rifle falls to the wayside as the Goose shatters, a few million little fragments splintering to the floor, into the air. Diamond confetti. The recoil travels the length of my arm and pain blooms like a waterbomb from where my neck and shoulder join.

He turns to me, grabs me by the bicep, and there are two loud bangs as his body goes limp. I feel his fingers loosen. I look behind him and Nico's eyes meet my own.

The music keeps playing elsewhere, there is a cacophony of blood-piercing shrieks and yells coming from over Nico's shoulder, behind double doors, but in this bathroom, with the fresh blood shed pooling under the bodies around us, I can only hear my own ragged breath and the elephant thump of my blood in my ears. He too looks a picture, like I've caught him wanking, or cheating, not having just riddled a man with a few bullets, snatched a life away between yesterday's bootcamp and tomorrow's parade.

No no no no no no no, I think again, except I've said it aloud, can tell I have from the way Nico's face collapses like a card tower felled by a breath. He's never looked younger, staring at me, big man with blood on his hands and a tremor in his lips. The agony in my arm is fading with the rush of adrenaline, a rush I can hear like surf between my ears. I tread back once, too shocked to be ill, too numb to be scared. I nudge into the two men, crouching behind.

91

Nico swiftly turns and confidently shoots into the empty corridor. I flinch but see it isn't empty; as he begins shooting, another armed man comes into view and falls before he can even register he's dead. Nico turns and takes a magazine from his pocket, swaps out his empty clip with a fresh one.

"Bear." His voice is gruff and quiet, admonishing a child, almost petulant. "Bear, you–"

My forehead meets his with a cracking noise. I feel it more than hear it, but it knocks me back with a ricochet. A field of stars in front of me, lightning tiger stripes. I see Nico's scrunched-up face. He grabs the edge of the skin, seething. "*Fuck! Bear!*" He shouts with bunched-up knuckles, clenched-down teeth. A small blossom of blood begins to emerge on his forehead.

I hurry past him, elbowing him the kidney, cherry on top. His knees buckle and he almost headbutts the basin. I step over the gun and I'm in the hallway before I chance a look back, see him pawing his way round. He sets eyes on me, then the gun, and I'm leaping over a body in the hallway and turning right into the smoking area.

I push out and there are bodies, bullet-riddled men whose lives were just petered out, scattered across the ground. My body is a battleground between freeze and flight, as I'm faced with the butchery of it all, a canvas of death smeared with blood and bodies, and I want to vomit and pass out and scratch this horror from my skin, but I have a racing heart and dirt under my nails that I need to clean, and now I have a name, a goal, and a terrible target it is, but I just need to flee and do *something* with it.

I rip my eyes from them, bring them straight forward as I head for the fire exit. I hear the stammer of gunfire hitting the wall behind me inside, prompts me to pick up the pace, hoof it until the slam of the fire exit locking behind me almost matches what I imagine is Nico pushing open the door to find me on the other side of the smoking area. "*Bear, come back!*" I hear him scream

Yellow industrial lights lead me towards the main road, and I beat across, dodging the still steady traffic, even gone one in the morning, until I'm certain there's enough distance and wide, public space between Nico and me. From the mouth of Glitch, I see calamity, stampede, an orchestra of bodies clambering over barriers, bleeding into the road. I can't stop, my breathing heavy. Camera men still. Idiots.

My vision begins to mottle and it takes me until I'm two streets over that I realise I'm weeping, that I'm still whispering disbelief to myself. Little breaths of *no no no* chugging out like car exhaust. I sink to my haunches halfway down towards Old Kent Road. There are sirens filling the air and the roar of a football crowd coming from Glitch half a mile away. I sniffle and I feel a madness building somewhere from my toe tips, coursing upwards as I cry until I worry I will implode. A madness built of rage or a snap in the mind, I can't nail it down, perhaps the two, but it floods me as I see Nico's face again, wipe another smear of blood away from my forehead. Bitter copper coats my mouth and I press my teeth together to ground myself, so hard I worry they will splinter and crack. I begin to stand with great effort and

Treading down the road, Black Prince Road behind me, lead in my feet, I hover over Nico's name in my phone as I dodge blindly the same faces as before, retracing my steps ad nauseum. I weave like a drunk. I can't compute, I feel myself buffering behind my eyes. I fumble with my phone, replace it in my pocket, take it out again, lather, rinse, repeat. Almost get hit by a car on Kennington Road as I skip across. My skin feels grimy, tight, and my stomach is an empty, a mossy well several miles deep. There's neon everywhere splattering me like some cheap Fresher's Week glowstick, and I fall sideways onto a bench outside some boutique bar whose name accordions wide and skinny through my hazy vision.

I'm fucked. I want to sleep, to fall into oblivion, a nice void of Vanta black and come out twenty-four hours later, on Saturday, tomorrow, not Friday again. July 3rd is laughing at me, snatching away my future every night. I'm approaching hour forty, I think, can't summon the energy to do the math. There's a server before me, trying to take an order, ask me if I need something, and I can make out a bouncer behind him giving me the eye. I tell him I'm good, get up and continue on my way to Jared's, the street stretching before me like a ruler of Blackjack.

There's a corner where the streetlight still flickers over an electricity box, and I usually pass through at this time, this stretch of road solitary as I aim for the long syringe of a building penned in with the moat of spaghetti junctions. I wobble towards it, and a figure comes into view. He advances on me. I fluster, my paranoia heightened by my strained mind, my fatigue doubling up on the tension rod that runs through my body. My fear conjures a gun, cached somewhere on his person, even as he takes form, is clearly holding nothing as he approaches. I stumble back, almost tripping over my own feet. Need to drop that habit.

He passes. I don't recognise him, but I am familiar with the look he offers me: crazy, insane, *you alright there, mate?* I huff out a long, billowy sigh.

Arriving at the syringe ten minutes later, ten minutes which felt like the longest wait at a doctor's office, I buzz up as a chime come from my phone. Moments later, I step out of the life and Jared's door opens, and Axel is there to welcome me, ever the hostess even in someone else's apartment.

"Hey, I need to borrow some shoes."

"I'm sorry, Bear. It happened so fast," he whispers, going off script. He looks flustered, harangued. "We didn't know he was coming."

I step past him, moving into the living space. "What you on about?" And I turn to see the crowd, the same groups as usual.

One extra person. A blip. Anachronism.

Stood with Jared and Andrew, Nico turns to face the door, his jacket still on. "Hey Bear."

He crosses the room. I feel Axel's hand at my elbow, his lips by my ear. "Andrew turned up five minutes ago, didn't mention he was bringing him." And then Nico is bearhugging me and squeezing hard enough to make a point.

He whispers, "Don't say anything to anyone." And then louder for the people in the back, "So good to see you." His hand ghosts over my own, fairy fingertips, and an imprint of his smell blankets my neck. The floral, appley scent lingers like a warning as he drifts back over to Jared. The rest of the room stares obviously, reverts back to normal scheduling as I turn to Axel. My limbs are stiff and my gut roils loud enough for Axel to size me up from belly to face.

"I thought you two were on good terms at least?"

I make my way to the bathroom, passing by Andrew and Robbie, who nod at me with concern in the eyes. Andrew grabs my bicep.

"He caught me outside, I couldn't say no, Bear." I hold up a hand, press through, fall to my knees by the bowl, and dry heave. It feels like I'm coughing up wire wool, nothing coming out except for spit and frustration.

My forehead touches the edge of the bowl, I don't even care about the hygiene of it all, or lack thereof, as I doggy-breath, crumpling little by little.

The door behind me opens and closes. I hear the lock bolt. Bleary-eyed, acrid fumes coming from the bowl, spiderwebbing my lips, my nostrils, I turn. Nico crouches next to me.

I flinch back, peddling my feet against the mosaic floor until my back hits the bath.

"Why are you acting to skittish?"

"Leave me the fuck alone."

He tilts his head and his curls loll to one side. "Why say something like that?"

"Leave me alone. Get out now."

"You're behaving … *weird*, Bear."

"You're fucking *dangerous*."

Nico's face settles as if a final jigsaw piece "And why do you think that?"

I swallow as he needles me until his gaze. Axel's sound system is pulsing around us, the bathroom echoing like an ultrasound. I turn from his gaze, my knees bunching up. "You need to go."

"Bear, why do you think I'm a danger?" He says each word with the weight of an anvil. Lays them out like surgical equipment. "Are you … going through something?"

I turn back to him, but my line of sight falls to his mouth. "I saw you. Do it."

"Bear, what did you see?" And that thin slice of terror grows wider and wider the longer I sit in the bathroom with him. I feel as if I'm toeing the edge of a precipice and in my sluggish state, I am unable to dredge myself away from it.

And then he says, "What did you see when you last reset?" And my eyes finally meet his again, and I'm the dumbest bitch in London because despite seeing him only a couple hours ago with a gun in his hands, despite the coppery smell of bloom mingling with the acrid piss stink in the bathrooms, the bleachy sticky tread underfoot, despite popcorn bullets still sounding in my head, the slam of doors, the screams of giants, I relax a little and feel a small part of my anxiety pass to Nico.

"How do you know my day reset?"

"Because my days are resetting. How many times?"

"Four, I think. Maybe five."

He reaches into his pocket, withdraws a pill. It's as big as a paracetamol and has a green tinge. Passes it to me. "Take this."

"What is it?"

"It'll keep you awake. What time did you wake up the first Friday?"

I hold the pill between my fingers, examining it. "I'm not taking this."

"What time, Bear?"

"Like, eleven?"

"AM?"

I fix him with the cattiest glare I can dredge up from my box of tricks. "Yes, Nico, I didn't have any work that morning. Let me live."

"So you've been awake like two straight days?"

"Feels that way."

"Then take. The goddamn. Pill." A beat. A softening. "I'm not going to hurt you." His hand inches a little closer to me.

Gooey warm honey pools in my belly and I place the chalky tablet on my tongue, dragging out the moment as Nico watches. I close my mouth, feel it slide down. Penny in a well. Regret looms larger than post-coital grief burgeoning on the horizon. Silence pools in the room, steadily, from the soles of our feet upwards.

"I didn't take part in the shooting," he throws out into the pool.

"You were carrying the gun."

"I know how it looks, but you headbutted me before I could explain."

"Explain you were a fucking *psychopath*."

"I was *stopping* a fucking *psychopath*, cunt."

A coil of annoyance winds itself into my belly, meets the penny, overtakes.

"What the fuck?"

"I tackled one of the attackers, stole his weapon. Used it on another bad guy."

"No, what the fuck is happening, Nico?"

"There's someone planning an attack at Glitch. Tonight."

"No shit," I begin to stand, feeling electric, renewed energy. Hand on knee, I rise and rest against the wall. Someone bangs against the bathroom door lightly and we barely pay it mind. "I mean, what is happening with me resetting the day?"

"*Us*," Nico corrects.

"Why is it happening?"

"I don't know,"

"You don't know?"

"I don't." There's a finality in his voice, heavy as a shipwreck.

"You just expect me to believe that? That you aren't a mass murderer when I caught you red-handed? That you have no idea why this is happening to me?"

"*Us*."

"I *don't* believe *that*!"

"Then why didn't I kill you?!" He blasts the question into my face and gives me pause. Nico Demetriou, calm and collected, perpetually mellow-headed. I dated him for an age and never saw him blow up. "Answer me that, Bear. If you're right, I could've taken a shot at you and those other two guys. But I didn't. I killed a bad man and tried to help stop … this but you had to be *thick* and just, fucking, react."

The knocking has stopped, likely in reaction to Bear's outburst. There's heat between us, pure anger and frustration, but some cogs fall into place behind my eyes.

"I'm going to need you to get over this." His watch beeps, a brief triple trill. "Because I don't have time for this. And we have to stop a mass killing."

A flat palm on the door to the bathroom, harder this time. A muffled plea. A beat and then I shake myself awake, feeling more myself. I make for the door, hand on knob, and Nico grabs me by the scruff of my chest.

"I'm going to Glitch. Now. And you need to follow me."

I start out the door, shrugging him off. "I don't need to do anything you tell me to do. You ended things, remember?" And I stalk into the room, past some man I don't recognise, aiming for oxygen, for space, for the balcony.

His words hit me in the back of the neck. "If you don't stop being so fucking selfish, people are going to die!" I can see in the black mirror of the sliding doors that his comment has parted the crowd, swerved heads all in his direction. I stop and turn around to see him heading for the front door. The music still blares, there was no record scratch moment, just Nico, jacket billowing out behind him like some cartoon cape, exiting.

There's a drop in the atmosphere, a hole by the door into which the entire party is staring, and then the song liaises into a different tune, a different DJ, and it shakes all the men from their reverie. I see Jared turn on his heel, drink in hand, phone in the other, nail me with a caricature of a look.

"Fucking batshit." He points his finger at me, phone still in grip. "You dodged a bullet there."

I left Jared's a little before the other guys, told them I was on the prowl before we hit up Glitch. Jumping in an Uber, I bought the ticket en route to the club, cut straight past the mile-long queue, head nod to Mike. I check my phone as I make my way into the main room.

Doesn't matter that I'm thirty minutes ahead of my own schedule, the venue is still a morass of bodies greasing up against one another. The same music looped over and over to ease the passage of chems through the body. I push through to find my way to the bar. Hello Ritchie, Caio, the hairdresser from *Gosh!*

"Those are new," Nico's words pour like honey into my ear. I still and then turn over my shoulder to see him looking down at my hands on the bar. There are a couple chunky rings on each hand, including a two-finger piece from some high street outlet I fished out of Jared's dresser. I pocket one hand, turn back to the bar.

"I want to make sure I'm ready for whatever."

"So another glass baseball bat?"

"Fuck off," I say, making eye contact with the bartender. "Bottle of water, cheers." I fiddle with my phone to load the payment. "You gave me an E."

"More or less. But I don't think it's kicked in fully."

"It's kicked in enough. I'm strumming like a bass."

"Good. You need to be alert."

I pay. As soon as we make our way to somewhere less crowded, a strobe lingers over his face and my eyes widen. Despite a roguish smile stolen straight from film noir, his face is looks like a punching bag. A black eye burgeons on the right side, his lip is swollen and cut, his cheeks blotchy with redness, turning purple under the turquoise lights.

"Nico—"

"Bomb's been taken care of." He grabs my hand and drags me towards one of the fire exits. We weave through a cloud of sweat, of tonic, of the unwashed, recently-fucked. We pause and my eyes move from Nico's focused face to the bouncer standing by the door. Nico's lips are moving but he's whispering, I can't hear him over the music. I'm about to ask him why we've paused but then, a minute nod to himself, we are walking forward slowly again. And the bouncer is moving from the door to the left-hand side of the room.

We move through the door, my panic spiking that there's an alarm, but nothing sounds, and then we're on the other side, a narrow grey-bricked wall with an overwhelming smell of bleach, cordial, and ale. We head left and through the warren of corridors, the wall threatening to cave in as we make it past the DJ booth.

"What's your plan here?"

Nico's voice takes a knife's edge. For the first time, he sounds angry. "Same as every day. Take out Rifle, get back to the dance floor, and then," he pauses talking as we reach the end of the hall. "I don't know. That's why I brought you here."

"To die a noble death?"

"Even if you do, you'll just reset." He's halfway out the door. Beyond, I can see a storeroom, shelves lined with bottles. My brain, however, latches onto his last words.

"No, I'll die."

"Yes. And then you'll reset. Like the last few times in the club."

"Nico, I've been alive when I've reset."

He swerves on me, the door still ajar. "You what?"

He releases his grip on my arm and it falls floppily to my side. I absently grab it, although it doesn't hurt, and picture perfect, I see myself, as if I'm stood stage left, and I look like a chastened child, and I redden. Despite my reputation, as Nico's words blanket my mind and take root like seed, I know I've been wrong, this entire time. Nico speaks with too much conviction, too much bass and testosterone. My words come out like royal icing, like autotuned pop music. "Very *close* to dying sometimes, yeah. But alive."

His eyes pierce. He doesn't move. I swallow, tapping my foot, and feel myself actually quaking slightly. I look away from him, my nose itchy, ready to sneeze.

106

The music comes through the walls in palpable waves but still he stares, unmoved.

"Bear, the moment before I wake up again, on the tube into Elephant and Castle, the last thing I remember is dying."

"I haven't died once, Nico." A roaring wave builds in my ears. "Except maybe the second night. Definitely not how this first started."

"The bomb?"

"The explosion."

"Yeah, I stopped it every night since then. And after that," he jerks a thumb behind him, to the open door, which widens slightly. "I deal with the—"

Pop pop goes Nico's neck, a splatter of blood spurting outwards, misting my face.

"You fucking liberty!"

Nico bellows at me on the approach to Jared's building. Hands in pockets at a distance, he now withdraws one and needles me with it. I've been idling outside for about ten minutes, waiting for him.

"Sorry for being such a *fucking* distraction. Spare a thought for the first time I've seen you *die!*"

He spreads his arms wide. "As you can see, I am not dead."

"You're enjoying this."

Nico begins to head down the road, and I follow. "I get the impression," he says, "that since you told me dying didn't reset you, that you've been elsewhere when the attack properly starts." Jared's flat is a little walk from the tube, but we have a couple of hours to ourselves before anything major starts.

"I've seen a couple."

"I saw the whole smoking area get shot up. Annihilated." From his pocket, he withdraws a pack of cigarettes, lights one up. A grey dragon escapes from his nostrils, snakes heavenwards. "It's not a competition, Bear, sorry. I'm not enjoying this at all. And I'm super stumped as to why this is happening to us." Under the arches, his voice echoes, bouncing from brick to brick. "Even for me, this is some weird shit, some sci-fi shit I can't wrap my head around. But the first time it happened, when I woke up on the tube, I tried to explain it to the people next to me, and that got me in trouble with the feds. I was raving, like, proper lunatic shit. Ended up running away from them across Leicester Square, got hit by a bus.

"Woke up back on the tube." He pauses minutely with frustration. "I figured out pretty quick that the window to act, for me to change something was too small to do anything except fix it myself."

"There's that superiority complex." I say, it falls out before I can think it over. It takes me a moment to register he is a few steps behind me, stood still.

"Oh, I'm sorry, am I wrong or did you not decide to attack the fucking shooter with some Grey Goose?"

"Because the cops wanted to know how I knew–"

"And I know what happens when you tell them the truth."

We stare one another down. He cocks his head at me until I concede, gesturing to keep walking.

"So I knew there was a bomb," Nico continues, "knew where, so I got to Glitch early, got Mike to let me in, and did some snooping. Found it in the boiler room behind the main bar and took it out the building." He pauses to take another long drag as we round the corner, the bright roundel of the station a beacon in the distance.

"You *deactivated* it?" I ask, breaking his rhythm but needing to know. Each word is softened clay, less brittle to touch.

He's still looking ahead, his cigarette a small thin orange nub. "I got shot. Back of my head at my guess." The very head he's shaking. Brings vomit halfway up from my stomach. "Woke up on the tube again. *Didn't* freak out this time, but knew where the bomb was, knew I was going to be shot. Every night since, it's been the same. I sort out the guy, the first shooter, and then I go looking for the others. The same." In what feels like the first time in many elastic hours, he looks at me. "Then I saw you, twice, and the first time, you looked so scared. But the second time, you were different. Determined. You attacked me.

"And that's how I knew."

We move through the vestibule that leads down to the platforms, tapping in and reaching the tube just as it pulls in.

"Because I was violent?"

"Because there was no reason for you to go off script. Nothing had changed. Stands to reason that you were the change. The variable. So," he huffs out a big breath, a cloud of relief, "I got off the tube when I reset and went to Jared's."

"How did you know I'd be there?"

"Andrew mentioned it that morning."

"You still talk?"

"We were friends before me and you, Bear."

"Traitorous bitch." I say, being drowned out by the screech of the tracks. I push my heel of my hand into my eye, mushing it as my drowsiness kicks up a notch. "You got another pick me up?"

He fishes in his breast pocket, pulls out a pill discretely as we step onto the train. It's at about capacity, we manage to wedge over the end of one carriage between the door and the seating. I put it under my tongue and dry swallow. He doesn't seem to join the party.

"Why are you not shattered at all?"

He turns from me, despite being pressed up chest to chest, stares over my head down the train. A few long seconds pass before he speaks. "Because I woke up at 5PM." And then, as a wan smile covers the lower half of his face, his eyes uncrinkled, unmoved, "Some of us don't have any work coming up."

The train bustles through the tunnel and the noise overwhelms the carriage as I try my hardest not to fix Nico with a questioning stare. I feel the chemicals begin to knead and scratch at my fatigue.

"I'm not going to pick that scab," I say quietly when the train pulls into the station.

"Thank you," Nico says, stepping off the tube, me following in the crush of people eager to enjoy their Friday night. "Now come watch me get a man to diffuse a bomb."

The main problem was twofold, the first being the shooters, emphasis on the last S, no matter how many attempts we made to get back into the main room. We tried a couple of different approaches, secreting stolen weapons down our trousers and coming in through the front, kamikazeing into the fray. Getting punctured like Swiss cheese wasn't working, resetting to have another go, it all felt impossible.

Number two on the list was time. The rush to get to the club and try and pre-empt any action was futile, a slap in the face of two very ragged men. Despite Nico's late rise on day one, by the eighth reset, he was yawning, face dropping with bags of weariness. We sprinted through warrens of London streets to get to Glitch, pull a fire alarm, get the throngs and hoards into the streets to relative safety, but we found out swiftly that this only triggered the carnage faster, water on a chip pan fire.

I leave Riley's flat, a double digit reset, with lead in my bones and a disco of fragments in my vision. I pull out my phone and leave a voice note for Nico, hoping he'll listen as he gets topside. To be sure, belt and braces, I leave a text too.

New plan. Meet me at The Volunteer.

The perks of being an attractive whore, the bartender has a quiet booth ready for me when I get there, upstairs, away from prying eyes. He offered a waiter to look after the table, I declined, just asked for a couple Black Cows and cans of Red Bulls. I neck two cans straight away. I can't remember the journey here, can't recall whether I Ubered here or not, probably not, The Volunteer isn't too far from Black Prince Road.

Paper cut-out man strides towards me, taking the shape of Nico around twinkly lights and deep navies and neons. He wears a mask two-parts curious, one-part scrunchy forehead, and I wave wildly as I crack open another can and decant over vodka. He takes a seat next to me, I scooch over to make room, and I pour him a vodka Red Bull. He takes the drink from me and places it on the table.

"What's the plan, Bear? You see something on the last reset?"

He watches me take a sip of my own creation in a highball before me, quirks an eyebrow as he takes out a pill, chases it with the can.

I spread my arms wide, triumphantly. "This is the plan, babe."

He stills, deer in the headlights. He wasn't moving heaps before but even in my delirious tiredness, I see him tense up, poised, coiled.

"What are you on about?"

Another mush to the eye with my damp palm. The only thing keeping me awake is the heavy music stemming from the floor above, and the thin string of willpower to try and get my words out neatly. I zone back into the bar, the booth, to see Nico has moved, his hand on my knee, a pill in his hand, poised by my lips.

"What you doing?" I ask, pushing him slightly. He presses closer.

"You need to take a pill," he says and my face collapses. I feel sad, used, betrayed by him in this moment. I can't understand why he isn't meeting me halfway, but instead trying to invade my body with pills and chemicals and force me in his direction.

"Noooooo," stretches out of my mouth. I push more forcefully now, moving to the other side of the booth. "No more pills, Nico. I'm *tired*. I want to sleep." I swipe at him, at his offering. I can't see him; my eyes are closed.

"Bear, stop dicking around."

"*M'not*. This isn't *working*." Another gulp of bubbling orange. "We need to stop."

His hand encircles my wrist, not tightly, but enough to convey impatience, the beginnings to threads loosening.

"Listen, Bear. You are delirious with exhaustion. You need to listen to what you're saying."

"We aren't good enough, Nico. We aren't fast enough; we aren't smart enough. We're talking now and they're starting up, getting ready. 'Ssembling." That last word runs together like a concertina, a slow car crash of English.

"Exactly!" Squeeze. "We need to get to Glitch and stop it."

"I can't. You can't. We need to try and get to Saturday, then–"

He rattles me. "*Bear!* You're being fucking selfish! We need to keep at this or there's going to be two hundred dead bodies come tomorrow morning!"

"There isn't going to *be* a tomorrow morning for us. Not if we keep going to Glitch and trying to save everybody tonight." My voice is strung-out, whiney, my mother would say I'm *whingeing*. "We can't go in there on the offensive because if we do, we're arrested, terrorists, whatever. And we don't have enough information to do anything else.

"Except wait. Let it happen. Reset tomorrow. Maybe. Or reset in a week, try and stop it with more information."

"That's not going to happen, Bear."

"What's the alternative?"

"We don't know what happens if we get to tomorrow." His voice is growing louder. "What if the day doesn't reset? What if our friends stay dead, Bear? You really want to do that?"

"Then we get them justice, Nico. We keep living because they can't."

"I'd rather try and save them."

I lash out, striking the highball to the floor. "I'm *tired*! Nico! I can't keep on like this." I can't remember the last time I opened my eyes. I can only feel Nico next to me, but I feel his fury, his impatience, the undulating waves of his desperation. "*Weneedtogetagrip*," I gum out.

I feel him stand, his knees hitting the table, the drinks sloshing. The ground feels wobbly under my own

115

feet as I move to look at him, my eyes parting only a little in the dim gloom. "I'm going." His voice is profound as a pebble tossed in a lake.

"*Yougonnatorturemeforever?*" My slurred words follow him like a slug across the floor, now filling with drinkers and staff, and down the stairs leading to the exist. I don't know if he heard me or not.

The sounds of sirens fill the room, the flashing blue coating the walls like dropped bubble gum ice cream. My eyes close heavily; finally.

TWO YEARS LATER

Someone asks us how we met, the question launched over the nuts and beers on the table, the sticky mahogany making our jumpers tacky with cider, with spilled Coke, and we both catch it with dog-like head tilts. Lightning bolt smiles strike our faces as we clock our synchronicity, and our fingers find one another on our laps, thighs pressed together like seven AM city commuters.

I take a sip, raising my eyebrows to him, wondering if he'll go with the truth or if an easy lie will come out. Aiden's smile takes on an edge as I see him weighing up between replies, looking at me minutely for guidance. It takes less than a heartbeat, but I see every minutia. He takes in a breath.

"At the gym," So he's lying. "He saw me struggling with hip thrusts."

"I bet he did," Aimee offers, tilting her wine glass a nudge in our direction. Laughs come from around the table right on queue. I cringe, performatively, chewing up the audience.

"I was! I almost broke my neck until he came over and repositioned me."

Declan leans forward. "And which position did he put you in?"

More laughs.

"Oh, fuck off, then," Aiden says, falling into my shoulder. I wrap an arm around him and nuzzle slightly. His hair smells like vanilla, matches the cider I'm drinking, and underneath, there's grass. There's always grass with Aiden; regardless of the season, he always smells like summer, like childhood water balloon fights under blistering sun, like baked pavements, like bare legs being whipped by wheat. He has this ability to transport me like a good book.

I kiss the top of his head. "His form has since improved." I say to the group. Aimee grins into her drink, Declan furrows his brow in a *sure, sure* gesture. Hazel and Maggie just stare dizzily at us, waiting for more. Aiden unfolds himself, grabs the roasted nuts, moves to take a sip of his bottle, and so the task befalls me.

"So yeah," I start, body beginning to buzz. "I just corrected him, and then we were doing the same workout, so we just buddied up." I look out the window and see snow beginning to fall lightly over the market square. The cement lions which stand sentry on either side of the town fall begin to freckle with white flecks. A tram passes, a smudge of green and grey, sounding its bell over the noise of the pub. I squeeze Aiden's thigh under the table. "And after a Nandos after the workout, we pretty much didn't stop talking." I look back at him, and he brings his attention to me. "That was … ten months ago?"

"Yeah, it was late January." His voice is a warm cup of mulled wine, spilling over with affection. Looking back to the girls and Declan, they wear sincere warmth on their faces. The quiet stretches out for a moment.

"I'm really glad I started training again."

"I am too. Immensely."

The conversations lulls into familiar comfort. The December night stretches on as Aimee and Declan updates us on their pregnancy, as Hazel tells us how her new job is going, all the saccharine, twee dross which fills in the spaces between conversations of import. It's a few comfortable hours before we leave the pub, treading down Nottingham concrete, Aiden and I towards the cabs lining on the High Pavement.

I think warmly and greatly about our cottage in Newstead. As my head makes contact with Aiden's in the back of the taxi, I close my eyes, letting the cider take over and lull me half to sleep. I can feel he's drowsy too, feel him slouch and mould into me as we are driven the ten miles or so from the city to the village.

There's a whole fortnight spread before us as we awake the next day. We peel ourselves from one another and I pad my way to the kitchen. It's barely eight AM and the light outside has barely cast away dawn, ribbons of white clouds peppering the slate blue sky like candy floss, and I move from room to room turning on the lamps until morning has truly arrived. Cold tile under my feet, the single-glazed windows rattling rapidly in the gale like the tiny ministrations of squirrels, I shrug my cardigan closer and boil the kettle. I go through the motions of preparing coffee; setting up a tray with a cafetière, choosing the grounds from the cupboard, flipping through my phone to find some mellow tunes to fill the house.

Aiden's arms find my waist and wrap around me. His lips land just under my left ear as we both stare out into the front garden. Frost crowns the grass blades like highlights, and I think how blessed and warm I feel him against me, feel him thickening against my rear, to have the house hugging me all around, smelling coffee brewing.

"What do you want for breakfast?" I say, tugging us out of our reverie. I turn to face him, find him shirtless, just the loose pyjama bottoms barely staying up around his lithe waist. A handful of months ago, Aimee called him "roguish" and it's the first word which pops into my head now whenever I see him, with his salt-and-pepper scruff to the scar which runs from the corner of his eyes to his jaw and cleaves his left cheek in two.

"Can we go to that cafe on the high street?"

"We spent heaps last night," I say, wringing a smile out and squeezing his triceps. "So I'm cooking today." I plant a kiss and move around him to begin, turning on one of the gas hobs and opening the fridge. All the stars have aligned without effort and we have all the trimmings for a full English each, so I begin to fry the bacon as I watch him out of my periphery take a seat at the wooden kitchen table and scroll through his phone.

"We need to visit my sister and her family before Christmas." His voice carries over the sizzle on the griddle moments later.

"I know we do," I say, walking over to him with a full mug of coffee and a firm kiss to the forehead. He smiles broadly at the latter. "We've got it pencilled in for the twenty-third, no?"

He flashes me his phone as I reach for the fruit bowl, shows me a page of a shopping website. "Do you think the kids'll like this?" Some wooden contraption that wouldn't look out of place in a doctor's waiting room.

"I think your sister's family already have enough junk." I take a bite of a banana. "I bought them some clothes, they're in the bag at the bottom of the wardrobe."

Aiden stands, making his way over to the counter by the window.

"I put two sugars in it …" I say over my shoulder as I return to the hob.

I hear the clean click of his mug being placed on the countertop, the soft shift of fabric as he moves to put his fingertips on the window.

"Babe, there's someone outside the gate."

I look behind me to see Aiden stood at the door, and my first thought is that he's letting in all the cold. I bristle but don't say anything, instead turning back to Nico. I do up the zip on my parka, take a few treads closer, so we're face to face with just the small gate between us. He too is bundled up but there's a frostiness about him, a thorniness, as if it would hurt to touch him. His hands are shoved in the pockets of his jacket. His hair hangs to his shoulders, curly still but dun, and his face is a stripe of beige against the black of his scarf and hair which protect him from the elements.

"I didn't change my number," I say, my voice being half-swallowed by the wind around us.

He wriggles his mouth out of his scarf like a cat trapped in a paper bag.

"My dad died." His voice carries, like a large stone thrown in a pond.

A balloon deflates somewhere under my breastbone. My shoulders sag and I feel my face fall with it. The wind howls around us and there's a clamour in the trees as a few birds take flight. I open my mouth to say something and my saliva stings as the chill catches it, it feels like a spider's web coating every plane.

He toes the grit underfoot, looks down as he worries it with his boot, the frost sounding above the wind.

"I'm sorry," I say, and he holds his head up like a puppy, his eyes wide as dinnerplates, brimming with tears against the wind. "I'm not letting you into my house."

The strings holding his neck up snap and his shoulders follow suit. I watched the line of his body go suddenly rigid and the path of his arm as he brought his hand out of his pocket and with it, a gun.

I barely have seconds to register his feet on the path down before Aiden is behind me. He has an arm across my belly, pushing me behind him, even as I refuse to budge, and he's looking between Nico and I at a rapid pace.

"Bear, no, get inside," he pleads, as Nico remains unmoved, just shivering slightly as he stares me down. Aiden and I, our arms almost battle as I somehow manage a closer step towards the gate, putting Aiden behind me.

"He's not going to hurt me." Aiden is persistent, trying to drag me back into the cottage. Dog with a bone, man with a sensible sense of preservation. I whip around to him. "He's not, he's posturing." Back to Nico. "You would've done it by now if that's what you wanted."

"We need to go back." Nico says and his words head straight for my tailbone.

"No, we don't." I try to put as much steel in my words as possible.

"Bear—"

"Aiden," I turn to him with bile rising steadily and my hackles at full attention. "I've got this."

"He has a gun!"

"And he won't use it!" I look back at Nico, who has the audacity to look annoyed. My face is heating up,

I can feel my ire in my fingertips. "He's just trying to make a point."

"Have I made it?" Nico grits out.

"Plainly."

"We need to go back, Bear."

"Your dad will still die, Nico. People die."

"I have *no one*!" He swings his arms dramatically and the gunshot cracks on the pavement to his left. We all flinch, Aiden snatching at my shoulder. Birds ascend from decaying branches, the snap of their wings against frost the only sound except the echo of the blast all around us. We all of us look at the ground where we roughly guess the bullet impacted.

"Fuck off, mate," Aiden spits with venom.

"You heard the man." I say.

Nico and I stare at one another for what feels like a day, feels like the sun slinks across the slate sky and we are falling towards dusk. His eyes shine and his breath is deepening, and his skin is turning more pallid as neither of us blink.

Finally, from him, "We're going back."

"Back where?" Aiden asks.

"No, we aren't!" I'm losing composure, advancing on him. "I have a life here, Nico! I have spent the last two years building something for myself in the ruin of that attack. I left London, left all that shit behind, and I–" I stop myself, and look behind, locking eyes with my beautiful man before turning back to Nico. "We found one another, and I have a life here.

126

"I'm sorry about your dad, but you can't–"

"This was just a formality, Bear." Nico's voice is eerie calm, a papercut across the sky. He steps back and I feel the coffee in my guts turning sour, roiling. He turns from me, and I chance a look back at Aiden, who looks panicked, confused. I watch Nico begin to idle, to loll back and forth a few paces away now from the fence. "I just wanted you to be prepared."

He brings the gun to his own head.

"No!" I shout, and I feel Aiden's fingers pincer my bicep as I try to run forward.

There's a crack, a déjà vu twig snap louder than an atom bomb ringing in my ears. I think I see the rose blossom bloom of grey matter leaving your skulls, think I hear my own mad barking as Riley's room overwhelms my vision and I stumble backwards, over familiar bedsheets in a golden-lit bedroom. I feel colder than a January evening as I fall to the floor, my vision spotty, and then, fade to black.

Pitty-pats like a cat pawing at an injured mouse grace my nose, my cheek as I swim heavenwards from a viscous and deep dark. I take in the sight of barely a man, kimono-clad waif, as I sit up, feeling the electricity of blood finding its rightful place in each avenue of my body. My ass feels numb. Blurred lines find grounding and become clear as do his gum-chewing sounds. I see his mouth moving and, as if a veil has been unsheathed from my ears, words take form.

"You hear me?" Riley asks, and I find myself nodding. He hisses out a smile, takes a pew behind on the bed's edge. "Babe, I knew I was good, but I've never made a guy faint from coming before." He leans back, fishes for something across the spread, throws me my underwear. He stands. "I'm going to get some ice for your head, you proper smacked the floor hard."

I manage to stand as he leaves the room, looking around. I'm still dizzy, it feels like an egg is slowly forming on the back of my skull, but I begin to dress. As I thread my leg through jeans, it washes over me.

I could scream.

I can feel my body begin to vibrate with ire, liquid rage, so palpable it burns the nerves behind my eyes and I begin to cry. I feel the tears pulls their salty underbelly down my face as I wrench on my shirt, restrain myself from unravelling into a tantrum right there. I swallow the excess saliva and try to steady the wobble of my lip. I reach into the pocket of my jacket, pull out my phone, even though I know, I know what I will read, don't know why I need confirmation.

Jul 3rd 2020.

Riley steps into the room and I push straight past him on the way out. There's a slate block of an injury on the back of my head but I don't even acknowledge the pack of peas in his hand, or his pleas, or his pawing, cloying fingers ghosting over my jacket as I pad down his stairs. Phone in hand, I furiously pound against the street as I push out into the very familiar scene of Black Prince Road.

Someone's shoved a sock down my throat, a giant cotton lump that no amount of swallowing seems to dislodge. I make my way down the street, looking for shelter, for a reprieve into which I can collapse. I find Nico's number on my phone, know it makes no sense to call, know he's seven floors below ground, thundering into Southwark Station or somewhere nearby on the Jubilee line, but I call anyway. It doesn't even connect.

I look up to find myself in front of a bar front, Glam Bar, and I look in to see familiar faces, all younger, all with the glow of health and good liquor. Creased with unravelled paper with momentary laughter lines. Swathed in yellows and red and neons and filtered through the silvery tendrils of cigarette smoke outside.

They're not vaping, I think, and catch myself as hysterical laughter threatens to boil over.

Jared's apartment building looms like a burnt-out matchstick above the wharf. It taunts me with amber-glowing eyes, hundreds of them, and the pulse of life coming from within. I know the routine, my place, my placement as a cog in the workings of the night. I see the same birds pass overhead, read familiar license plates as the same cars pass under the inky night sky.

I toy with my phone. In between the flares of anger which scream like white noise, ricocheting around the cavern of my skull, Aiden's face comes to the front. Carved porcelain like a statue, classical looking. He comes into focus in waves that pepper my chest with anxiety, with a cloying panic. And his voice, I hear it like a continuous hum. Like he's taking a breath somewhere over my shoulder, readying himself to speak. It rolls my shoulders into knots and my breath comes out staccato.

What would you do? I think of him, my man who is lost, two years in a future I can't revisit, that may no longer exist. I don't understand the mechanics of any of this, tried immediately after the blast to find a source of this endless looping. Found myself on the brink of madness, chasing every article I could find down rabbit holes. And the only thing which prevented me from plummeting down the cliff face of my mania to my own demise was an Irish accent wrapped in a schoolteacher.

The dread creeps in like a cold front, meeting my extremities first before coaxing its way beneath my skin and burrowing close to my heart. I feel like I want a cigarette, an impulse I haven't felt in years, and my phone is in my hand before I realise it.

Nico hasn't shown.

I look around and try and parse his familiar silhouette. I don't see him coming from down under the bridge, and he should be here, and now I've got needles in my veins, great big urchin puncturing me from within. I begin to get antsy, head away from the building, away from the phantom party sounds. I swear I can hear screaming coming from twenties stories up, cheers of revelry and debauchery.

My phone startles me as it chirrups in my grasp. I look down, my face bathed milky in its glow, and see Jared's name flashing on my screen.

"Jared?" I ask, even though I know it's him, and he isn't a ghost, he just isn't dead yet. His name, however, feels heavy and acerbic on my tongue, a lump of coal. And when he speaks, I'm a lanced boil.

"Bear! It's so tragic!" I see him slipping over a fictional chaise-longue. There's music blaring in the background, chart, Top 40 tunes from yesteryear which provide stark contrast to his mournful voice. "Bear, it's Nico."

Eyes wide open. I stop walking. I look back, up at the skyscraper, and I'm suddenly in the room upstairs. I wonder how he slipped by me, made better time when every other night has seen him arriving a couple minutes after me. I turn on my heel, being to tread back towards the building, and it's only from the hard smack of my steps that I realise rage is funnelling back into every crevice of my body. Gone is the worry, the curiosity, and it was been replaced with the same anger that announced itself in Riley's room.

"What about him?" I huff.

"I'm so sorry, Bear. He's dead."

Ice bucket challenge on my pulsing hot rage. A handful of emotions are trying to press through all at once. A million scenarios flood my brain and I lose vision briefly, machine gun blinking. There's a whomping noise coming through the phone but words lose their form as they exit the speaker, disappear like vapor into the night sky. My ankle gives way a little and I stumble, and then, I speak.

"There's a body?"

"Weren't you listening? They found him on the tube coming into town. They called me because I was in his recent calls, they said."

"I just saw him," I say, my voice the smallest trickle of gravel falling from my mouth.

"He was shot, Bear."

"What?" But of course.

"I'm sorry. It looks like he did it to himself."

"On the tube?"

"Bear, there's no gun, apparently, but it looks like suicide."

Suicide.

Not accidental, not murder.

I find myself swaying back, away from the building. My feet are taking me somewhere against my will, my body a hostage to the pavements of London.

"Are you still going out?"

There's a choking sound on his end. "What? No, of course not!" And then he begins to splutter as I picture tears clogging up his eyes, turning them into mushed raspberries.

He's back to whomping. My phone is in my pocket before I feel his mouth sounds fading to black, and after a brief glace at my watch, it finally dawns on me that I'm beelining for Glitch.

Blood on the bridge of my nose, I catch myself in the aluminium reflection in the stock room. A cut between the eyes, and three more siblings to it on the knuckles of my right hand. This is more difficult to do solo, I'm running behind schedule, minutes falling between my bloodied fingers like raindrops, but I'm ploughing through.

Number one is dead on the floor somewhere between me and the ring road. There's a bassline passing through me like fishing wire as I count down the hallway guy, number two, and Mr. Stockroom, number three.

Copper is painted on the inside of my nostrils, cloying and metallic, and my ears ring with the sounds of gun casings and the butchery thud of my fists connecting with flesh.

And boxing it all in, the only thing threatening to unspool my body and spill madness onto the floor, is the panic of not knowing how tonight will end with Nico's body laying on a gurney somewhere, not resetting, not trying to save the night once again.

I stare myself down. My hair is mussed, my jacket torn from the tussle with Numero Uno. There's a black spot in my ear, a blip that sounds like tinnitus, and I briefly think about how I have no intention ever of listening to this fucking music ever again, and then, I check my watch. I crouch. Five minutes and change before five swipes of *Rendezdude* are shot up, aerated. I lick my dry lips and close my eyes.

There's a gun in my hand and a small paring knife in my pocket, the blade stained with lime juice. The tip of the gun reaches my lips as I bring my hands together, poised to pray, planning my next move. By now, I have as many of the chess pieces as I've encountered lodged in my brain, and the next move has always been chaos. I run through the scenarios Nico and I went through years ago, trying to parse out directions, create a strategy. I feel like I'm drowning in the time rushing past me and I'm trying to breathe, trying to think of anything that could turn the ebb of the tide of tonight's events in my favour, to shed less blood.

A thought crests over me.

Scarlet-faced, claret-marred, and too exhausted to register the pain, I stand.

I'm almost out on the dancefloor when I notice the electrical box beside the door leading back into the club. Pistol in hand, I open the box and, with my free hand, nudge open the fire exit. Once a spider's silk of melody, the DJ's full oeuvre came barrelling through and hit me as I flipped all the switches I could see, hoping the end result would be desirable.

I step out into the club, almost greeted by a wall of flesh, to see the whole main room flooded with the house lights. The men look like spooked deer, bright eyed, glassy with narcotics, chems, even with the music still pumping away. The DJ mustn't have twigged yet. I feel as though this diversion will bring with it a sped-up timeline, feel like the deviation from the normal routine of a club night will provoke the attackers to act sooner, so I move as fast as I can.

I take the pistol and fire it up in the air.

Pop pop pop.

The bullets connect to the ceiling and flakes of charcoal paint shower me as the music dwindles low and then abruptly stops. The crowd pressing around me fans out like a rainbow and then they all of them begin to retreat, slowly at first, and then with gusto. Heads turn like gorgons over their shoulders as bare-chested boys and bondaged men lurch towards the exits. I'm faced with tight-jawed Insta models and a haunting harmony

135

of high-pitched squeals and low bellows. The stomp and shuffle of hundreds of men sounds like violence, like carnage, but it brings a manic smile to my face as I watch them flee.

Gun metal flashes to my right as I watch someone swimming upstream, approaching me through the throngs. He's dressed more conservatively than most of the men, which is to say he's dressed, and from his side he brings up a gun, twin to the one I carry, stolen from a dead man's side. He's two steps away, wearing a look of anger smushed over a confused expression, and it's in his valley of hesitation, as he assesses and calculates, as he does that math at there being more than one attack on Glitch tonight, that I find I am quicker.

I aim my gun towards his shoulder and fire. The contours of his face change like tempestuous seas in the seconds it takes for the bullet to leave the magazine and find its way through his body. He falls to the floor and I don't hear his cry over the continuous stampede before us.

Adrenaline keeps me floating on a cloud, masking my pain and wounds like candyfloss and aloe. The dancefloor is half cleared and I can through swinging double doors that people are fleeing into the smoking area. Usually, we see a couple of shooters coming down the steps to the main floor, and so I swing around to aim at the double doors.

Like clockwork, the doors slam open and I manage to get one shot off at the one on the left. He falls as his companion, armed with an automatic weapon, begins emptying his magazine in my direction. I run back on myself, aiming for the DJ booth, the bullets hitting around my ankles and toes like raindrops. The ground erupts, small volcanoes, shards of wood and debris exploding around me as I push through the agony and dive to safety. I feel a hard slice of metal scrape across my cheek as I come to a halt against the base of the decks. The attacker keeps on shooting a halo around me, I can see the wall above being blistered with cracks, and I quickly unload my magazine to check what ammunition I have.

Snapping it back into place, the gunfire ceases and I crawl around to try and peek. Through foggy reflections against the wall, I can see a silhouette coming down the centre steps with eyes trained on the DJ booth. There's a sleekness to him, panther-like, a swagger in his tread. The barrel of the rifle looks venomous, looks dazzling in the mustard glow of the house lights. I lean back and look at my knees, contemplating my options. I wasn't lousy with them: either would put me in the open, the fire exit back on my right, the doors to the toilets on my left, both some distance across the floor.

My heart speeds triple time. Salt coats my blood-cut lip. I wipe my sleeve across my eyes, trying to make my vision less blurry.

I ascend and serve inelegantly, Bambi on ice, to my right. I catch the ice pick glint of his gun pursuing me as I swivel to aim my own gun and fire.

137

Bullet holes perforate the wall behind me as I sprint to the side, eyes trained on the shooter, my finger working over the trigger, a countdown of remaining bullets in the back of my mind. My aim is poor, but so is his as we both begin to circle. Both on level footing, I now see he isn't so tall, and isn't too broad.

He's slight and petite almost. A bullet grazes my shoulder and he stops shooting. He flicks his fringe out of his eyes as he lowers his arm, as I lower mine. I seethe.

Eyes widening like apertures.

I know I look feral.

I know him.

"You."

He steps forward, his face moving from manic and fear to exhaust and, it takes me a moment to name it, to register it, but then, with his crooked smile splitting his face in two, with his shoulder set with surety, I recognise it as victory.

He says, "Me."

"*HotBot90?*"

A fragment of his composure slipping. "*My name is Riley!*" A couple of cracks as he raises the gun against and shoots over my shoulder to the wall behind.

We are both panting. The room has emptied out. Behind him, I see the double doors slightly open and a couple of faces in there, peering in, but there's an eerie quiet, a significant silence as the vast hall of this once-popular theatre is now void of almost everyone except Riley and I. Pebbles in a lake.

"Why?" I manage to heave the question out like dropping carrier bags on the counter.

"Because you cunts are a plague."

"You what?"

He takes a step forward and I flinch. Three years ago, I would think nothing of it, having fallen victim to the violence of shooters one through three, but tonight, with Nico's body laying somewhere in London with no change of waking up, my fear of death is rekindled. With his tread forward, Aiden's face floats before me, his lilting voice warm against my ear, and I panic at the thought of never seeing him again.

The panic must show.

"You look fucking terrified," Riley says with glee. Another step and I hate myself for stepping back. I have a couple of bullets left, I think, but his weapon looks lethal and the magazine still robust with carnage. "You the one who stopped the bomb?"

"Yeah," I say as confidently as I can. "What was the plan there? Kill yourself?"

"It wasn't the atom bomb, *Bear*." He says my name with derision. "Just enough to do some damage at the front door, stop too many of the smackheads getting out."

"So you hate gays that do drugs?"

"I hate cunts like you and your friends," he swoops his gun around his head at the empty auditorium, "swanning around like you're fucking gods."

"What the fuck are you on about?" I don't want to poke the bear, but I'm lost.

"You fucking circuit gays!" I can see the spittle leave his mouth. "Cookie cutter, steroid-taking, slutty guys who think you're better than everyone because you fly to Mykonos every year and you don't have to queue for clubs like this! You treat people like shit, you won't dare make friends with anyone who even look slightly different than you. God forbid you're caught in the company of someone with more than ten percent body fat." He sniffs a little, runs the sleeve of his gun-holding arm across his nose.

"So that means death to all gays?"

"Not all gays, just the muscle Marys like you and your mates."

"There were over five hundred guys here tonight. You really think they're all the same?" My spine is heating up, the nape of my neck roiling with electricity as pain seeps back into every pore. "And so what if they are? They aren't hurting anyone."

"We aren't disposable!" His voice echoes around us. "The guys you fuck, that you use, we aren't just for your personal use. You go around sleeping with us but won't give us the time of day for a coffee or anything." He's red-faced now and looks ill, looks sweaty and tired. I take a step to my left and he brings up his gun as a reminder. "You fucked me earlier today and then bailed. Left me without so much as a kiss. Didn't even remember my name.

140

"We have feelings. You can't be so selfish."

He was right. I did see him today.

Every muscle in me halts. My face feels freshly Botoxed. I daren't blink.

"So you're the leader of this ... cause?"

"You bet." All five feet four of him looks smug as.

"I managed to take out all three of them before having this chat with you."

"So there's still a couple more out there," he nods his head backwards towards the general direction of the front of the club, "dealing with you parasites. No worries."

I think of Aiden, somewhere in the country; of Jared, and Axel, and Andrew.

I smile, knowing they're all safe.

"What're you smiling at?"

I say a silent prayer to whatever is out there.

"You were a terrible fuck, Riley."

I register his constipated rage, his lithe loose arm swinging up, and the aggressive chewing of his mouth as he spits out invective that's smothered by the firework pop of his gunfire.

And we meet again, Riley.

Softer, glowing, sweaty for all the right reasons. I trace the line of his spine listlessly as I pull out of him, and mouth along minutely to the words and sounds he makes. There's a queer comfort in the familiarity of the scene, of this room, in this flat on South Vauxhall Road.

Riley falls forwards and I see a flash of Jared's bullet-riddled body.

Riley writhes at the covers, pooling them at his feet, and I hear the cries of hordes of men as they fall underfoot, as they are stricken down my gunfire.

Riley looks as me with blissed-out eyes, concealing a venom and contempt; pouts with bruised and swollen lips like tulip petals, and I feel Aiden's lips on my own.

He stares at me and I realise a beat too long has passed as I kneel on his bed, still dripping, my chest rising and falling with a building panic. I close my eyes for a moment and sigh, trying to level my breathing, talk myself off of the ledge.

"Sorry, I zoned out there, what did you say?" My voice tremors minutely, and I wait to see if he reacts.

"I asked if you were going out tonight?"

I step off the bed, search for my underwear, my jeans. "Um, yeah, I was thinking of heading home."

I feel him sit up, readjust, as I bend and begin dressing. I turn to look at him, and his head is tilted up at me.

"I pegged you for a guy who'd be heading to Glitch."

"I think you'll find I just pegged you, actually," I bite the lip of my smart mouth. Still, he laughs, and rolls over to grab his phone from the bedside table.

"That's true."

I look around as he taps away and for once, take in the room. I look at the spines of the books that dot the shelves of the bookcase by the door, and stifle a shudder seeing names that point towards extremism. I see how messy the room actually is, from a patch of mould by the window overlooking the railway arches and the crumbs and shredded envelopes on his desk.

"Why'd you assume I'd be heading to Glitch?"

He stops typing and looks at me like he wants to devour me, eyes blazing with hunger and arousal. "You're muscular, a good shag, and a handsome. Kind of a given."

"Huh." I bring my top over my head and make my way over to the desk, fingers ghosting over the paperwork for a moment. I rest on the edge and put on my shoes. "I garden."

"What?" He tilts his head.

"I garden, I discovered over the past few years I enjoy it and I'd sooner be in the garden than a club."

"Okay…"

I put on my jacket and get out my phone. "Just saying. Don't judge a book." I stand in the doorway and look at him, this small boy, so full of anger and resentment, so lethal. "Maybe, Riley, if you thought about how people are more complex than just what you see on apps … I don't know …" I really thought I had an ending, but all I can do is watch his eyes go round as dinner plates as I turn and step out of his bedroom and make my way to the streets of London.

As soon as the breeze of the city hits my face, the call connects.

"Fire, police, or ambulance?"

"Police please." I say.

TWO WEEKS LATER

Giggles of glee glide towards me on the warm breeze from the Market Square to my perch outside a coffee shop. I sit in denim shorts and a slightly sheer shirt, my ankles crossed, my coffee cup empty next to a book I just finished. The sun is blistering and the short-clad, bare-chested guys I keep seeing are going to wake up lobsters in the morning, but there are many hours of drinking which stretch between now and then.

In black and white, I read more about the arrest of Riley Moncrief, of his five collaborators, how he folded like origami as soon as the first flashing blues graced his apartment and gave them up. How cattily they tossed each other under all the buses and how still, a fortnight on, stories are contradicting one another. July 4th, Pride in London, the news broke in the morning and it was all anyone was talking about as they marched, drank, partied. Axel and Jared couldn't get enough gossip whereas Andrew was sincerely emotional at the idea of someone coming for kin.

After more than a few hours in a police interview room, I spent July 4th sleeping, eating, calling my family, and, finally, planning a trip up to the Midlands.

I lay down my newspaper on the bench beside me, pocket my paperback, and head into the street. I wander up the road and down a couple of side avenues before I find myself at my favourite place in the city, a small indie bookshop tucked away from the main roads. I can't fathom how it's stayed open, how it will remain open at least three years from now, when I've never seen it with more than five people in at once, but it's a stalwart of the community, as the corkboard dotted with yoga brunches and music lessons can attest to.

I enter and the little bell chimes. Across the way, the bookseller turns from his laptop on and looks up, makes eye contact.

"Hello you," he says, his voice as melodic as I remember.

"Hey again," I say, blushing to my neck.

"More cozy crime? Finished that Christie?"

"You're learning too much about me."

"All except your name, apparently?"

I find I've stepped clear across the empty shop so there's only the counter between us.

"Bear." I hold out my hand.

"Bear?"

I smile wider, I haven't stopped since I saw him.

"Just go with it."

"Will do," he says, and shakes my hand. "I'm Aiden."

ACKNOWLEDGEMENTS

I started this novel during NaNoWriMo 2019, and as 2020 draws to a close, I'm finishing it.

Thank you to Jazz, my Palm Springs cheerleader; to Chris Spiteri, for the blankets and the mezcal; to the tweeps on Twitter who had to read every single lamentation and nerdgasm I had when writing this.

To South East London; to the men who inspired it, from Clapham to Streatham to Vauxhall.

And to Imre, my heart. *Szeretlek, édesem.*

Author Bio

James Berry was born sparkling and glittery in 1990 in Mansfield, England. Now based in London, his writing is everything he likes about himself made prose: very queer, often weird, and pretty verbose. He was recently published in Thuggish Itch: Hospitality, a horror anthology by Gypsum Sound Tales.

He can be found on Twitter @ConcernedGoat. Don't ask.

Printed in Great Britain
by Amazon